THE CURÉ OF ARS

THE CURÉ
OF ARS

The Priest Who Outtalked the Devil

Written by Milton Lomask

Illustrated by Johannes Troyer

IGNATIUS PRESS   SAN FRANCISCO

Published by Farrar, Straus & Cudahy, Inc.
A Vision Book
Reprinted with permission of Farrar, Straus and Giroux, Inc.

Cover art by Christopher J. Pelicano
Cover design by Riz Boncan Marsella

Published by Ignatius Press, San Francisco, 1998
ISBN 0–89870–600–9
Library of Congress catalogue number 97–76848
Printed in the United States of America ∞

CONTENTS

JEAN-MARIE

JEAN-MARIE VIANNEY walked up from the valley where he had settled his sheep for the night. It was beginning to rain. Within the walled-in farmyard on the hilltop the first patters made a sharp, jarring sound.

Jean-Marie ran. He skirted the pond in front of the house, pulling up short on the stoop to kick off his wooden shoes.

The door was open. In the yellow-lit kitchen he

could see his mother going about her work. He watched her take some onions from under the cupboard and carry them to the big center table. Her shadow, cast by the fireplace, flickered over the opposite wall—over the dressed sheep hanging there, over a row of fish strung up to dry near the open stairway door.

"You are alone, Mama?" He stepped in.

Madame Vianney turned with a start, fixing him with eyes as soft as the rest of her was rough and ungainly. "So it's you, Jean-Marie." She fairly barked the words. "Yes, I am alone." She seated herself at the table and tackled the onions with a long knife. "Only alone is not the word. I have been deserted."

"Deserted, Mama? How could that be?" Jean-Marie stood by the hinged shelf under the window. The shelf was high. He had to stand on tiptoe to reach the soap lying alongside the washbowl. "When I left this morning, Papa said . . ."

He got no further. "Papa said!" His mother picked up his words in a mocking shout. "Ah, yes! This was the day your brother and your sisters were to stay home and help with the spring cleaning. That's what your papa told them this morning. But then what happened? Perhaps you can guess."

"No, Mama. What did happen?"

"Our neighbor dropped in, our Monsieur Vincent from down the road. He was on his way to Ecully. And why to Ecully?"

"Why, indeed, Mama?"

"Because there was a herd of cows for sale in Ecully today. That's why. And what kind of cows, Little One? Cows made of gold, to hear M'sieur Vincent tell it." Madame Vianney's shoulders shook, for she was always the first to chuckle at her own wit.

Jean-Marie chuckled too. Cows made of gold indeed! Only Mama could think of anything as delicious as that.

"Ah, yes, of gold!" Madame was still laughing. "And when your father heard about the cows, what did he do?"

"I suppose he wanted to see them too."

"Exactly, Little One. He, too, must go to Ecully. But is he content to go alone with M'sieur Vincent? Ah, no. Never! Your brother and your little sisters must go with him. And so . . . !"

Madame Vianney's tone changed abruptly.

Her voice sank to a whisper. Rather it sank to what she thought was a whisper, for no one ever had been able to convince Madame that hers was an unusually loud voice. Even her whisper filled every crack and corner of the big kitchen.

"*Ma Foi!*" She clapped a hand to her mouth. "The racket I make. It is enough to wake the dead."

She leaped to her feet and hurried across the room. Softly, very softly, she closed the stairway door.

Jean-Marie stared at her with suddenly widened eyes. "Mama!" he pointed ceilingward. "We have a guest in the best bedroom?"

Madame Vianney nodded vigorously. "He came before your father left this morning. A little breakfast, then right to bed. He's sleeping still, I daresay. Unless, of course, my racket has awakened him, thoughtless creature that I am!"

"Is it another priest, Mama?"

"Yes, Little One."

"I'm glad!"

"Glad!" Madame Vianney sped to the cupboard and grabbed a plate. At the fireplace she fished hunks of bacon out of a blackened pot and ladled them onto the platter. "Glad! You will not feel glad when you see this one. The man is so tired. Ah, how worn and tired his poor face is!"

She placed the platter, generously filled now, on the center table. "No doubt the poor man is hungry. You will take him his supper."

"Yes, Mama. I shall be happy to."

Taking a yard-long loaf of bread from the cupboard, Madame Vianney laid it on the priest's platter. Then she got a bottle of wine.

"There now!" She turned, facing her son, who was still standing at the far side of the table. "Jean-Marie!" Her manner was suddenly stern, almost sad. "Come here."

Hurrying around the table, Jean-Marie stumbled over a low stool. Madame Vianney's hands went to her hips. She leaned back, shaking with silent laughter.

"Jean-Marie!" she cried. "You are the clumsy one. If

you were in the biggest field in the world and if there was only one object in the whole field, you would stumble over it. Would you not, my Little One?"

And, Jean-Marie having reached her, she lifted him with her strong hands, kissed him, and planted him on the stone floor again. Then she seated herself on the table bench and motioned to him to sit beside her. "One second before you go", she said. "I have a question to ask you."

"Yes, Mama." He sat down on the bench. Mama's face, he could see, was solemn again. "Jean-Marie!" She spoke softly now. "Whenever a priest stays with us I see you following him around. I see you looking at him with your heart in your eyes."

Madame Vianney paused. She uttered a sigh as sharp and loud as one of her whispers. "Tell me, Little One," she went on, "would you like to be a priest yourself when you grow up?"

Jean-Marie hung his head. For a second he had trouble finding his voice. It seemed to have got lost. "Oh, Mama", he said finally. "I . . . I . . . Is it wrong of me, Mama? To have such dreams, I mean?"

Madame Vianney smiled. "My question, Jean-Marie? What do you say to my question? Is it your wish to become a priest?"

"Yes, Mama."

"Ah!" Madame Vianney looked away, far away. Her next words were directed to herself. "Only eight years old and already he dreams of becoming a man of God!"

Jean-Marie tugged at her dress. "You have not answered *my* question, Mama. Is it bad of me—what I wish?"

"No, Jean-Marie." Madame Vianney sighed again. "It is not bad. Only . . ."

"Only what?"

"Only it is not easy being a priest in France now. You know how it is with our beloved country. Surely Papa has told you."

Jean-Marie nodded. Yes, Papa had told him. He had told him how, shortly before his own birth, bloody strife had torn France in two. The Revolution of 1789, Papa called it, because that's when it had all started. The French people had revolted—some of them, anyhow. They had cut off the head of King Louis the Sixteenth, and of his queen, too.

The new rulers of France, Papa said, were godless men. In Paris they had chased the priests out of Notre Dame Cathedral. They had set up an idol there, an idol they called the Goddess of Reason. Now here in Dardilly, and in all the other towns of France, the churches were closed. Mass was said in remote barns. Priests lived in hiding like that poor, tired man in the best bedroom upstairs. The priests had to go about disguised as carpenters or cooks. If they were caught, they were sent off to be galley slaves on French ships. Sometimes they were sent to a prison camp in a far-away country called Guiana.

"Yes, Mama", he said. "I know how it is."

"Well, then!" Madame Vianney leaped to her feet. "You must think hard before making a decision. You must think hard and pray. Now, off with you. Our holy guest will be starved. But wait . . ." Madame Vianney snatched an iron oil lamp from the table. She lighted it at the fire and handed it to her son. "There! Can you manage everything?"

"Of course."

Jean-Marie tucked the wine bottle under his arm. He held the platter in one hand, the oil lamp in the other. His mother held the door for him. He could hear it closing softly behind him as he climbed the steep stone stairs.

2

THE SOLDIERS

IN THE BEST bedroom upstairs Jean-Marie could hear
the rain dancing on the far side of the beamed ceil-
ing. He put the lamp on a little table near the bed and
set the priest's supper beside it.

Then he stood for a moment looking at the sleeping man on the bed—looking at him, as his mother
had just said, with his heart in his eyes.

He was a small, bony man with a small, bony, tired
face. Old or young? Old, Jean-Marie decided, judging

by the gray in his hair and the deep lines that every-where latticed his features. But just then the priest opened his eyes, and Jean-Marie saw that he was not old, only tired. The dark eyes that fixed themselves on Jean-Marie were soft and young.

"Your supper, M'sieur", said Jean-Marie. He almost said "my lord", but corrected himself in time. Only bishops and suchlike, Papa had told him, were ad-dressed as "my lord". You said "Father" to a priest who belonged to a religious order, simply "Monsieur" to one who didn't.

The priest sat up, shaking himself a little, and hoisted his legs over the edge of the bed. It was a high bed, and the young priest had thrown himself down on the thick coverlet. His thin legs did not quite reach the floor. He sat there blinking at Jean-Marie. He had a blue kerchief at his neck, and he wore the rough clothes of a carpenter. Nothing about him marked him a priest—nothing, that is, except the round shaved spot at the top of his head, the tonsure of a servant of God.

Jean-Marie knelt, and the little man on the bed gave him his blessing. "Another boy", he said as Jean-Marie got to his feet.

"Another . . . ?" Jean-Marie was puzzled, but only for a second. "Oh, I see what you mean. When you came this morning my brother was here."

"There was another boy certainly."

"That was my brother, François Vianney. I am Jean-Marie Vianney."

"I am glad to know you, Jean-Marie. I am M'sieur Balley." Monsieur Balley's mild eyes went to the food on the table beside him. "You have brought me my supper, I see."

"Oh, yes, M'sieur. You must be hungry."

Monsieur Balley shook his head. "It is a lot of food", he said. "You will share it with me, perhaps?"

"Oh, no, M'sieur. I will have my supper downstairs when Papa comes. He and the others have gone to Ecully."

"I see." Monsieur Balley blessed himself. Then, tearing off a hunk of bread, he dipped it into Madame Vianney's good gravy. "And when I came this morning, Jean-Marie," he said, "where were you?"

"I was in the fields."

"A worker already, eh?"

"Papa lets me tend the sheep. Sometimes Gothon goes with me."

"Gothon?"

"That was the littlest girl you saw this morning. Her real name is Marguerite, but we all call her Gothon. It's a silly nickname, isn't it?"

"It's a charming one." Monsieur Balley ate slowly, his quiet eyes on the food before him.

Jean-Marie edged toward the door. "If you need anything more, M'sieur?"

The priest looked up. "If I do, I will call you."

"You will not forget my name?"

"No, Jean-Marie."

"Good. I will leave you to eat in peace, then." But at the door Jean-Marie hesitated. Coming up the stairs an idea had struck him. It had seemed a wonderful idea at the time. Now he was not so sure. Perhaps M'sieur Balley would think it ridiculous. "M'sieur!" He turned back to the priest.

"Yes, Jean-Marie?"

"I have an idea. It might be of help to you. Would you—would you care to hear it?"

"But of course. What is it?"

"Well, M'sieur, you know how things are. Sometimes the government soldiers come into the village. They search the houses. Suppose we didn't see them in time? Suppose they caught you here?"

"Well, then!" With a flick of his hand Monsieur indicated his rough garments. "In that case I am a hard-working carpenter."

"But your tonsure, M'sieur!"

"My tonsure!" The priest's hand went to the bald circle at the crown of his head.

"Don't you see, M'sieur? If the soldiers see that, they'll know. Only religious men shave their heads that way.

"I have a hat, Jean-Marie. I'll put it on."

"And if the soldiers tell you to take it off?"

"Well, then!" Monsieur Balley shrugged. "My goose is cooked!"

"But it need not be. We can hide the shaven spot."

"Hide it? How?"

"With ashes from the fireplace downstairs. Don't you see? There's gray in your hair, and the ashes are gray. I could get some. I could rub them in and then . . ."

Jean-Marie stopped speaking, suddenly aware of the smile forming along M'sieur Balley's thin lips. He hung his head. "I'm sorry, M'sieur; I'm being very silly."

"Oh, no, my boy!" Monsieur Balley was on his feet. Crossing the room, he rested a thin hand on Jean-Marie's shoulder. "You are being thoughtful and kind. Thoughtfulness and kindness are never silly."

"You *do* think it's a good idea?"

"A wonderful idea, my boy. Get the ashes!"

Jean-Marie flew down the stone stairs. He was delighted. To think that he, Jean-Marie, had thought of something that would be of help to the holy man! He could hardly wait to tell Mama.

But Madame Vianney was not to hear of his idea that evening. Papa and the children had come home. The others had gone to their rooms to change clothes, but Papa was at the fireplace. He was taking off his wet boots and talking excitedly to Mama.

He leaped to his feet, seeing Jean-Marie, and came stalking toward him. He was a big man. His eyes, large and blue like Jean-Marie's, were set deep under a heavy brow. "Our guest upstairs, Jean-Marie. He is all right?"

"Why, yes, Papa. Is there something wrong?"

"I'm afraid so. We saw soldiers camped in the forest as we left Ecully."

"Are they coming this way?"

"Who can say? Now, Jean-Marie, listen carefully."

"Yes, Papa."

"You know where the two roads meet about a mile from here?"

"Yes, Papa."

"Good. There's a small hill by the fork of the road and a hedge. Hide yourself there and keep a sharp eye."

"I will indeed, Papa." Jean-Marie, grabbing his hat, made for the kitchen door.

"And, Jean-Marie," he heard his father shouting behind him, "if you do see soldiers, take the shortcut home. And mind you waste no time about it."

Monsieur Vianney's last words were lost so far as Jean-Marie was concerned. He was already through the courtyard gate and running hard across the rain-swept fields.

By the time Jean-Marie reached the fork in the road, the rain was smashing down. It was a true spring shower. At intervals cracks of thunder ripped the sky. Blue and yellow lightning flamed over the nearby hills.

Jean-Marie made a cave for himself under the hedge. The thunder growled, the lightning flashed. The small boy, resting snug and excited on his knees, didn't mind. He thought of the Bible stories Mama was always telling—of the creation of the world, of how God had created everything, so, of course, everything was good. As for the rolling thunder and the lightning, what were these things after all but God at His grandest?

As Papa had said, the little hill above the fork was a good place to watch. Or, more exactly, it was a good place to listen, for between lightning flashes the night was pitch dark.

Not being one to waste time, Jean-Marie said his prayers. He had no rosary beads. He had owned a set once, a beautiful wooden rosary given to him by his aunt in Ecully, his mother's sister. It belonged to his little sister Gothon now.

Jean-Marie remembered the day little Gothon had asked for the beads. She had asked for them with her very first real words. He remembered Mama looking first at Gothon and then at him, and then saying, "Give them to her, Jean-Marie."

He had given them to her, of course. When Mama said "do", you "did"! But how he had sobbed as he handed the pretty rosary to Gothon.

Afterward Mama had explained. "It is never too early, Little One," she had told him, "to learn self-denial."

Still later Mama had made it up to him. She had given him, for his very own, the carved figure of the Virgin that had stood for generations on the kitchen mantle.

Jean-Marie's hand went to the pocket of his blue shepherd's smock. The little figure was there, of course. It always was. He held it up and breathed a prayer. "You will keep the good priest safe from harm, will you not, Blessed Mother?"

Another prayer was forming in his mind when he became aware of a sudden and stabbing increase in the rain. At the same time a different sound reached his ears.

Voices! Men's voices. Rough voices, coming closer now and closer. He crawled to the edge of the hill. Just as he reached it, there was a roll of thunder like the report of a thousand guns. A flash of lightning exposed the road coming from Ecully.

He saw them then—a straggly group of men carrying pikes and guns with bayonets attached. Obviously they were headed for his own village, for Dardilly. His parents' farmhouse would be the first stop on their route.

He darted down the hill and across the fields, taking the shortcut home. The soldiers would take the road. He could beat them by fifteen minutes, even more if he ran fast enough.

He ran as hard as he could, slowing to a walk occasionally to get his breath, speeding up again as soon as possible. Sailing into the courtyard, he forgot about the pond. He was wading through it before he noticed it. His stockings were plastered with mud when he entered the kitchen.

Papa was pacing the room, Madame Vianney sitting by the fire. She screamed as he dashed in. "Jean-Marie, what have you done to yourself?"

"It is only water, Mama. The pond. I forgot about it!"

"Forgot about a whole pond? *Ma Foi!*"

She was on the verge of telling him to change his stockings at once when Papa broke in.

"Soldiers, Jean-Marie?"

"Yes, Papa. A gang of them headed this way."

"Upstairs with you at once, then. Take the priest with you to the woods. And when you come back, you know what to do?"

"Yes, Papa."

"If the soldiers are still here, say nothing. I'll answer their questions. And take this." Monsieur Vianney shoved a lighted lamp into his son's hands.

The lamp splashed crazy shadows over the plaster as Jean-Marie hastened up the steep stairs.

Monsieur Balley was still sitting on the edge of the bed. He had dozed off. His head came up sharply as Jean-Marie entered.

"Ah, Jean-Marie", he said. "You have brought the ashes?"

"The ashes!" Jean-Marie had almost forgotten. "Oh, no, M'sieur, there is no time to cover your tonsure now. The soldiers are coming, and I must hide you in the woods."

Jean-Marie opened a door leading to a balcony and

an outside stair. He blew out the lamp and left it on the little table. He directed the priest in a loud whisper. "It is dark outside, M'sieur. Hold tight to the stair rail."

They hurried down the steps, across the courtyard and two open fields. At the edge of the wood, Jean-Marie halted.

"It is very dark in the forest, M'sieur," he whispered, "but I know the way. If you will be good enough to put your hand on my shoulder . . ."

"I shall do that, boy."

And so they proceeded in the thick woods along a winding path. Deep in the woods Jean-Marie halted again. "We turn off here, M'sieur", he said. "Hold tight, now."

They were in the thick underbrush. A few steps off the path and again Jean-Marie halted, this time between two tall birch trees.

"Here, M'sieur." He dropped to his knees, feeling about with his hands. At length he found it—a board thickly covered with underbrush. He lifted it, exposing a hole in the earth big enough to hold a man comfortably. "It is not a pleasant place, M'sieur. But it is quite safe. I will come for you the minute the soldiers have gone."

Jean-Marie felt the priest's hand on his arm. "I am grateful to you, Jean-Marie", he said.

"It is nothing, M'sieur."

The priest crawled in. Carefully Jean-Marie replaced

the brush-covered board and hurried back to the path. Regaining the open fields, he set out quickly for the farmhouse.

3

A LONELY WORLD

A S HE STOOD on the front stoop removing his wet
shoes, Jean-Marie could hear the soldiers stomp-
ing and shouting through the farmhouse bedrooms.

Madame Vianney sat knitting near the kitchen fire;
Papa rested in the big armchair. He looked up as Jean-
Marie entered. His right eye closed in a broad wink,
and he put a finger to his lips. Jean-Marie nodded ever
so slightly. He smiled to himself, hearing Mama's noisy
sigh of relief.

"And now, Jean-Marie," she said, "as soon as the soldiers come out of your room you will remove those wet clothes."

Madame Vianney spoke as calmly as if nothing unusual were going on, as if a dozen soldiers tramping through the bedrooms upstairs and through the smaller rooms beyond the kitchen were an everynight occurrence.

Two of the men came out of the room where Jean-Marie slept with his brother, François. At the same time another four came clattering down from the best bedroom. Only two wore uniforms. The others were dressed like French farmers. In truth, the army of the new government in Paris, like the government itself, was only a mob—a hit-or-miss ragtag of untrained youths.

"Well, Sergeant!" Monsieur Vianney addressed the taller and leaner of the two men in uniform. "Are you satisfied?"

The sergeant grunted. "We find no priest hiding in this house, if that's what you mean."

Monsieur Vianney shrugged. "And what made you think you would?"

"We hear things, M'sieur. We have our spies." He gave Monsieur Vianney a saucy look. "You have hidden priests here in the past, have you not?"

"Do you really want to know?"

"But of course."

"Then put your question to your spies."

The lanky sergeant grinned. Then he frowned. He leveled his bayonet in the direction of Jean-Marie. "We have not seen this one before", he said. "Just who is he?"

"He? Why he is Jean-Marie, of course!"

"Another son?"

Monsieur Vianney started to reply, but his wife broke in ahead of him. "He is not a daughter—obviously!"

The sergeant gave her a look, half angry, half amused. He grunted again as three more men, all in uniform, came out of the room where Jean-Marie's three sisters slept.

Their young faces puzzled Jean-Marie. Indeed, the faces of all the soldiers puzzled him. After all, they belonged to the army of the godless government in Paris. Somehow he had expected them to look dark and evil. On the contrary, they were much like—well, much like his fellow villagers. The lanky sergeant bore a striking resemblance to the handsome Monsieur Vincent, their nearest neighbor. And the smaller youth behind him, the one with the torn coat, reminded him of his brother François.

Papa was speaking again, addressing the tall sergeant. "Well, now," he said, "you have searched the house. You have searched the barns and the stables. And you have found nothing. So! How about some wine to cheer you on your way?"

The sergeant turned to his men. There was much

talk among them, much laughter. Then, in a cheerful stampede, they seated themselves on the benches along the center table.

Jean-Marie saw his mother signaling him with her eyes. He scooted into his room, closing the door behind him.

As he did so, he heard his brother François speaking from the bed. "Have they gone, Jean-Marie?"

"No, not yet. But it is all right."

He peeled off his wet clothes and put on dry ones. Then he waited, standing close to the bedroom door. He could hear the talk in the kitchen and the laughter and clinking of glasses. Once he heard his father's voice rising above the others. "Ah, yes," Papa was saying, "it is a crazy world our France has become."

More talk, more laughter, more clinking of glasses. Then a loud, scraping noise told Jean-Marie that the soldiers were leaving. He waited a little more, making sure they were gone before he opened the bedroom door.

Papa was standing on the front stoop. He joined him there, taking his hand. The rain had slackened. He could make out the soldiers' heads bobbing along the far side of the farmyard wall. They were trudging northward toward the center of the village.

His father spoke in a low voice. "Be patient now, Jean-Marie. Our priest must stay where he is until they are well out of sight."

"But it is so uncomfortable in the woods, Papa."

"Do not fret yourself. Our holy man has been through worse. He is a brave fellow, that M'sieur Balley."

Ah, yes! Jean-Marie nodded to himself. He wondered if, when he grew up, he would be . . . But there, who could hope ever to be as brave as M'sieur Balley?

"Tell me, Papa," he said, "do all these young soldiers really believe there is no God?"

His mother, stepping out on the stoop behind them, answered his question.

"Right now they think they do. But they will learn. They and their leaders will soon enough find out."

"What will they find out, Mama?"

"That it is a lonely world without God!"

4

THE FOOL OF THE FAMILY

I T WAS IN the spring of 1794 that Monsieur Balley
hid for a night in the Vianneys' best bedroom. Early
the next morning he said Mass in a barn on a remote
section of a neighboring farm. Then, carrying the
little sack holding his altar stone, his missal, and his
tattered vestments, he set out for a nearby village.

Jean-Marie accompanied him as far as the edge of
the hill on which the farmhouse stood. The rain had

ceased during the night. The morning sun, now fully risen, was blinding bright.

Standing on the crest of the hill, shading his eyes, Jean-Marie watched the priest trudge down the path leading to the ravine known as the Valley of the Singing Blackbird. He watched him cross the creek, stepping from stone to stone. On the far side Monsieur Balley turned and waved. Then he disappeared into the forest.

Sighing to himself, Jean-Marie turned homeward. The words his mother had spoken the night before ran through his mind: "It is a lonely world without God!" How long, he wondered, would France try to live without Him?

He would know the answer in time. For six years the churches of France were to remain closed. Many more priests came and were hidden in the best bedroom. Some nights large groups of people came, for the French Revolution of 1789 had done harsh things. In the beginning the revolutionary leaders had promised "liberty, fraternity, and equality" to the common people. In the end it was the common people who suffered most. Many saw their houses burned to the ground by rioting mobs. Many lost all their earthly possessions.

The homeless were everywhere, trudging the country lanes. Occasionally a group of them wandered into the village of Dardilly, lying among its hills and vineyards in the rolling country of southeast

France. The homeless refugees came at nightfall and headed for the Vianney farmhouse. They had asked questions along the road. The Vianneys, they had learned, would give them food and shelter.

On such nights, after all the refugees were fed, Jean-Marie and the other children helped Madame Vianney tidy the big kitchen. First they wrung out the refugees' damp clothes. They hung them on ropes stretched near the fireplace. Then Jean-Marie, grabbing the twig broom, swept the stone floor.

Exciting days, busy days. There was always more than enough work to be done around the farm. Jean-Marie cultivated the vineyards or helped tend his father's small flock of sheep. His sister, Gothon, usually accompanied him to the pasture.

Together they headed for the Valley of the Singing Blackbird, the flock at their heels. Some of the neighbor boys drove their sheep. Jean-Marie led his.

"Sheep are scaredy creatures", he explained to Gothon. "It's kinder to lead them. Besides, if they are happy, they eat more. If they eat more, they get fatter. The fatter they get, the more money they bring on the market, and that pleases Papa." He gave his sister a big wink. "And you know how Papa is", he added.

Gothon laughed delightedly. Yes, she knew how Papa was. Papa considered himself a sharp businessman indeed.

Almost two years younger than her brother, Gothon was a round and pretty child with her mother's firm features and dark eyes. Her pigtails went flip-flop as she danced along beside her brother; she stopped occasionally to admire a flower or talk back to a cawing crow.

A day in the fields passed quickly. Sometimes Jean-Marie knitted. Like all French farm boys he made his own stockings and sweaters. Sometimes he and Gothon played nine-man morris, a game played with rocks and sticks on a sort of chess board drawn on the earth. Moving their "men"—the sticks and stone—from hole to hole along the "board", Gothon and Jean-Marie each tried to line up three men in a row.

When Gothon made her first row she shouted with pleasure. Making a row meant that she could remove one of Jean-Marie's men from the board—any of his men, except that so long as he had other men left, she could not take a man from one of his rows.

Seconds later, she made another row. This time she gave her brother a sharp glance. "Now look, Jean-Marie," she said, "you must do your best. Sometimes I think you *let* me win!"

Jean-Marie shook his head vigorously. "Oh, no!" he said. "I wouldn't dream of doing that."

But, as a matter of fact, he often did. After all, he reasoned, Gothon was the younger. Then, too, he liked the way her face lit up when she removed all the men from the board and so won the game.

Sometimes, taking clay from the creek bed, Jean-

Marie made a shrine for his little statue of the Virgin. One day he and Gothon staged a procession. Jean-Marie took the lead, holding the Blessed Mother high above his head. They marched along the creek a hundred yards or so and back again, singing old religious songs at the tops of their voices.

At eight, Jean-Marie had been small for his age. Later he shot up rapidly. At eleven he was a tall, raw-boned lad. Life in the open had roughened and darkened his sharp features and faded his large blue eyes.

The neighbor boys laughed at his walk. "He walks like a duck", they said.

In truth, Jean-Marie's feet turned out in a comical way. Even his mother had to smile, watching him flapping across the farmyard en route to the fields.

The other boys laughed at his piety too. "He is forever blessing himself", they said. "And when he prays, he doesn't see or hear anything around him. At such times you could steal the clothes off his back."

The boys played tricks on him. Seeing him on his knees in the vineyard, they sneaked up behind him. They took his pruning shears and his hoe and hid them in the tall grass. It amused them, later on, to watch him running about with a bewildered face as he looked for the missing tools.

Once, Jean-Marie caught them taking his equipment. His only reaction was a smile—a crooked, wistful smile that lighted his faded blue eyes.

In far-off Paris the revolutionary government—the

republic, as it now called itself—passed a law about schools. Every French child, the law said, was to receive an education at the expense of the government.

The law made no change in the life of the Vianney children. In fact, it made little change in the lives of French farm children generally. For generations, France's only teachers had been priests. Now, of course, priests were outlawed, so very few schools were opened because there was hardly anyone to run them.

Monsieur Vianney, sitting before the kitchen fire one winter evening, broke into a low chuckle. "What a joke", he said to his wife. "The government passes a great law. Everyone is to have a free education. But then the government kills half the priests and hounds the rest into hiding. So there is no one to instruct the children, and the law is worthless! What a joke!"

Madame Vianney frowned. "I see nothing to laugh about", she said. "It is no joke for a boy to grow up without schooling." Her eyes were on Jean-Marie standing nearby. Slowly they drifted to Catherine, his eldest sister.

"Catherine!"

"Yes, Mama." Catherine looked up from her sewing at the big table.

"You know those books in the bedroom upstairs? Get them. You are going to teach Jean-Marie how to read."

The lessons began that night and continued throughout the winter. Jean-Marie's texts were a large volume called *The Lives of the Saints* and the smaller *Imitation of Christ* by Thomas à Kempis.

He did not learn rapidly. Months later he was still having trouble reading the simplest words. Nor was Catherine a patient teacher. A tall, handsome, highstrung girl, Catherine was a quick learner herself.

"*Ma Foi!*" she exclaimed one night after Jean-Marie had ploughed his way, with many mistakes, through a paragraph of the *Imitation of Christ*. "You have no memory, Jean-Marie." She stamped her foot. "You comprehend nothing. Yes, and finally, you are a dunce. You are the fool of the family!"

Her outburst brought Madame Vianney hurrying from her fireplace chair. "Catherine!" Madame's voice soared to its highest. "You must not say such things to your brother."

"Oh, please, Mama!" Jean-Marie spoke up before his mother could go on. "Please don't scold Catherine. She is only speaking the truth!"

"The truth!"

"Why, yes, Mama. I *am* a dunce. I am the fool of the family."

"*Enough!*" Monsieur Vianney's heavy voice clamped down like a lid on his son's words. Climbing out of his armchair, the stocky farmer joined the little group at the table. Catherine started to speak, but her father silenced her with a shake of his head. "You will listen to me now", he told her. "All right, you have some skill in your brains. But your brother, this dunce, as you call him, he has skill *here!*"

Monsieur Vianney spread his heavy, rough hands in front of his daughter's face. "Do you understand me, Catherine? Being able to do things with your brains is good. But being able to do things with your hands is just as good. And with his hands Jean-Marie is very good!"

Jean-Marie hung his head. He could feel his face burning. He didn't mind being called a dunce, the fool of the family. What he did mind was being praised. Praise frightened him. Praise, he knew, sometimes made people vain and overproud. What if he should become like that? He shivered at the thought and hoped his father would say no more about him.

But Monsieur Vianney had only just started. "You understand what I'm saying, Catherine?" he went on. "In one day on this farm Jean-Marie does more work than all of the rest of you put together. And better work at that!"

He punctuated his statement with a sharp nod and stepped closer to the table. "So suppose we forget the books", he continued. He took the volume Jean-Marie still held in his hands and picked up the other volume from the table. "Suppose we put them both back where they came from. After all, a good farmer like Jean-Marie—why should he fill his head with needless learning?"

Monsieur Vianney strode toward the stairway, the two books in his hands. He did not get far. Two quick steps brought Madame Vianney to his side. Snatching the books from her husband, she returned and dropped them on the table.

"Sit down, Jean-Marie!" she ordered. "Sit down, Catherine! The lesson will proceed!" With that, Madame Vianney, after a scathing look at her stunned husband, hurried back to her chair by the kitchen fire.

Monsieur Vianney continued to stand by the stairway door, gazing at the back of his wife's head.

From the bench at the table came Jean-Marie's low, uncertain voice reading again—this time more easily—the paragraph that had started all the fuss:

"Grant me, O Lord, to avoid the flatterer. Wisdom teaches us not to be misled by pleasant words. Heeding only the word of God, we go on safely in the way we have begun."

5

THE LATIN LESSON

J EAN-MARIE was fourteen years old when the great
news came. The Vianneys' neighbor, handsome
Monsieur Vincent, brought it.

The Vianneys were at supper. It was a spring
evening. A soft breeze brought the murmur of bees
into the big kitchen.

Papa had just finished saying grace when Monsieur
Vincent burst in. Monsieur Vincent was an excitable
man at all times. He was a regular windmill now. His

hands punched and tore at the air as he shouted out his news. He was so full of it and so eager to tell it that he talked faster than anyone could follow. When he had finished, there was a stunned silence. Anyone entering at that moment would have thought the people in the room were statues.

"But, M'sieur!" Papa Vianney pushed back his chair. He was suffering still from a touch of rheumatism first felt during the winter. With sighs and grunts he got to his feet. "What are you saying?" he inquired. "It is hard for us to take in. You say this Corsican fellow—this Napoleon Bonaparte—is now ruler of France?"

"He is head man, yes. He has been named First Consul."

"And you say he does not object to the churches?"

"He has opened the churches. Do you not comprehend?" Monsieur Vincent waved his long arms. "All is as it was in the good old days!" he shouted.

"Oh, thanks be to God!" Madame Vianney's voice rose in a wail. She lowered her head, her lips moving in prayer.

That night Jean-Marie had trouble getting to sleep. Monsieur Vincent's news was hard to believe. It was hard to believe that any day now the Angelus would once more ring out over the fields.

As a matter of fact, no church bells had sounded in Dardilly or in any of the surrounding villages for many months. The leaders of the revolution had done their work thoroughly. They had killed, or sent out of the country, nearly two thousand priests. For two years there simply were not enough to go around. Most of the country churches remained closed.

Then one summer Sunday in 1802, the little stone church in nearby Ecully opened its doors. The older Vianneys, Papa and Mama, went to Mass, riding in the cart behind the family donkey. The young people walked, taking the shortcut across the fields as far as the fork in the road.

Jean-Marie walked with his eldest sister. Catherine was a young woman now, fresh-faced and sprightly. As they tramped along, she talked happily of a forth-coming event. "What good fortune", she said to her brother. "To think that I can be married in a church after all. I wonder who he is."

"Who who is, Catherine?"

"The new priest at Ecully, of course. I've heard no mention of his name."

"Nor I."

"Oh, well, we shall find out soon enough."

When they did find out, when Ecully's new priest stepped into the sanctuary, Jean-Marie's eyes moist-ened. The scenes of a memorable night flashed through his mind. The little priest now genuflecting at the foot of the altar was Monsieur Balley—the very priest Jean-Marie had hidden in the woods the night the soldiers had come to Dardilly eight years before!

As they left the church after Mass, Madame Vianney took her son's arm. "And now, Jean-Marie," she said, "you must drop in at the presbytery." She pointed to the priest's small house next to the church. "It will be interesting to see if Monsieur Balley remembers you after all these years."

Jean-Marie begged off. "I will call on the good priest some other time", he said. "Everybody is trying to see him today. The poor man will be worn out."

"Indeed!" Madame Vianney spoke dryly, giving her tall, thin son an amused glance. "You are certainly the shy one", she said. "Oh, well, no doubt it will pass. I was shy myself when I was your age."

Jean-Marie had to smile. It was hard to think of his blustering, good-natured mother as having ever been shy. He gave her a long look. Had Madame Vianney happened to glance his way at that moment, she would once again have seen her son "with his heart in his eyes."

"Next Sunday, then", she was saying. "Next Sunday, perhaps, you will call on Monsieur Balley."

"No doubt", Jean-Marie said. But he did not call on the priest the next Sunday or the next.

The weeks passed, the months, the years. Off and on the Abbé Balley, as the pastor of the Ecully church was officially called, visited the Vianney farm. He came several times during the preparations for Catherine's marriage. On every occasion, Jean-Marie was away, doing his work in the fields or in the vineyard.

The winter of 1806 was bitter cold. Monsieur Vianney's rheumatism worsened. For days on end he was forced to hug the kitchen fire, leaving the work of the farm to his sons.

As spring came on, Madame Vianney, true to an old custom, paid a short visit to Daybreak, the farm on which her sister Margaret lived, on the outskirts of Ecully.

She returned at noon three days later. Jean-Marie, working in one of the barns, spied her crossing the farmyard and shouted, "Welcome home, Mama. And how is Aunt Margaret?"

"Aunt Margaret is well, thank you. And how is my good man, your father?"

"He is better. He is working today in the lambing yard. Did you have a good time in Ecully?"

"I did, and I have something important to tell you. Come in when you have finished what you are doing."

"In a few minutes."

"Good. And on your way, Jean-Marie, bring some pine sticks for the fire."

When Jean-Marie entered the kitchen, Madame Vianney was already hard at her work. She was stirring the simmering contents of the blackened pot hanging over the fire. As Jean-Marie deposited the wood on the hearth, she lifted the spoon to her lips, sampling the stew.

"*Ma Foi!*" She made a wry face. "Three days away from my own hearth, and I have forgotten how to cook. Herbs, Jean-Marie. Fetch me the herbs."

At the shelf under the window Jean-Marie washed his hands and dried them vigorously. Then he fetched the herbs from the cupboard. Madame Vianney sprinkled them into the stew and tasted it again.

For a second she hesitated, screwing up her face in deep thought.

"Wine!" she decided finally. "It needs a bit of wine."

Jean-Marie fetched the wine. His mother doused the stew liberally and sampled it. This time she nodded. "Ah!" she said, smacking her lips. "I have not lost my touch yet."

Jean-Marie returned the wine to the cupboard. "You had something to tell me, Mama?"

"Yes." Madame Vianney seated herself on a small rush-bottomed chair and motioned Jean-Marie to a nearby stool. "Great things are happening in Ecully", she went on. "The Abbé Balley has opened a school."

"A catechism school?"

"Oh, not that. He has had a catechism school from the beginning. This is a school for priests."

"For priests?"

"Yes. It seems there is still a great shortage. The Abbé Balley is getting a few boys ready so they can attend the higher seminary in Lyon and become priests." Madame Vianney gave her son a searching look. "You remember the evening we hid Monsieur Balley upstairs?"

"To be sure."

"Then no doubt you remember the question I put to you that evening."

"Yes, Mama."

"Well, then!" Madame Vianney shot the words like bullets.

"Well, then, what?"

"You know what I am asking. You wished then to become a priest. Well, you have had time to think, time to pray. Is it still your wish to become a priest?"

Jean-Marie tried to speak, but his voice failed him. He could only nod.

"Good!" Madame Vianney was on her feet. "You say your father is in the lambing yard?"

"Yes, Mama."

"Well, then, we shall talk to him there." Grabbing her shawl, Madame Vianney sailed through the kitchen door. Jean-Marie followed.

Papa was bending over a sick lamb. He straightened up slowly on seeing his wife and son, and nodded.

"So you are back, my dear", he said to his wife.

"Yes, I am back." Madame Vianney planted herself in front of him. She pulled her shawl somewhat closer, for there was a touch of chill in the spring air. "Yes, I am back," she repeated, "and I have a request to make of you."

"A request?" Monsieur Vianney grunted. "You have seen something pretty in the shops of Ecully. You want to part me from some of my money, from some of my hard-earned sous."

Madame Vianney nodded. "I want to part you from many of your hard-earned sous", she said. "Abbé Balley has opened a school to train boys for the priesthood. I want you to send our young man." She nodded toward Jean-Marie, standing tense and uncomfortable behind her.

Had Madame Vianney asked her husband to burn his barns he could not have looked more startled. His mouth fell open and, for fully a minute, he stood staring at her, speechless. "My good woman", he sputtered finally, finding his voice. "If I heard you correctly . . . !"

"You heard me correctly, M'sieur. I want you to send Jean-Marie to Abbé Balley's school."

"Send Jean-Marie away!" Monsieur Vianney had his full voice now. "Send away the best worker in all of Dardilly!" he roared. "Madame, have you gone mad? Do you not know that our country is at war? Do you not know that this Napoleon—this man who calls himself emperor now—thinks of nothing but battles and more battles?"

"What has Napoleon and his silly battles got to do with Jean-Marie's going to school?"

"What indeed! You know that I cannot do much work any more because of my rheumatism. You know that Napoleon must have soldiers, that any day now François, our oldest boy, will be called into the army!"

"So François goes. And then what? Cadet takes his place." Cadet, Jean-Marie's youngest brother, had been born during the same year that Monsieur Balley had hidden in the best bedroom.

"Cadet!" Monsieur Vianney snorted. "It would take a dozen Cadets to do the work Jean-Marie and his brother do around here. Besides"—and Monsieur Vianney shot his wife a sharp and sudden glance—"is it not dreadfully expensive at Ecully?"

"A few francs a month for tuition."

"Not to mention board and lodging. Jean-Marie cannot attend school in Ecully and live here. It is too long a trip to make twice a day."

"Jean-Marie will live with his Aunt Margaret in Ecully. I have already spoken to her. She would be delighted to have him."

"Delighted, eh? A worker like Jean-Marie around the place! Who wouldn't be delighted! Besides . . ." Again the sharp glance from Monsieur Vianney's blue eyes. "What is this all about, anyhow? Since when has Jean-Marie the desire to be a priest?"

"Since when, indeed! Since he was four years old and you and I found him kneeling in the cowshed praying to the little statue of the Holy Mother."

"Childish fancies."

"Fancies then, maybe, but convictions now!"

"Convictions that you have put in his head, no doubt!"

"No! I have not influenced him in any way. If you doubt that, ask him. Ask him!"

Madame Vianney stepped aside, leaving father and

son face to face. The older man's eyes blazed. "Well, Jean-Marie! Is it true what your mother says? Have you indeed the desire to be a priest?"

With difficulty Jean-Marie found his voice. "Yes, Papa", he said.

"But it is out of the question. Out of the question!" Forgetting his rheumatism, Monsieur Vianney gave the gate of the lambing yard a vigorous kick, opened it, and stalked away.

His wife ran after him, and Jean-Marie after her. They followed him across the farmyard into the kitchen.

At the washbasin Monsieur Vianney scrubbed his hands, muttering to himself. Crossing the room, ignoring his wife and son, he lowered himself, grunting and groaning, into the armchair.

Madame Vianney stood over him. "Well, then, my good husband," she said, "have you spoken your final word?"

"Yes, Madame. I have."

"Then I will say mine. Do you remember what Monsieur Groboz said about this boy?" Madame Vianney, with a quick gesture, indicated Jean-Marie.

"I do not even recall a Monsieur Groboz. Who is he?"

"One of the priests we hid in this house during the troubled time."

"We hid so many."

"You should remember Monsieur Groboz. He was

the priest who heard Jean-Marie's first confession. Right here in this room, it was. Over there." Madame Vianney pointed to the corner where the tall clock stood near the hinged shelf under the window.

"Oh, yes. And what was it Monsieur Groboz said about Jean-Marie?"

"He pointed at him one morning and he said to me, 'This one is for God!'"

There was a silence, a long silence. Jean-Marie could hear the sheep bells tolling in the distant fields.

Then, in a voice that was low for her, his mother spoke again. "I understand how it is about the farm, my good husband. Difficult times face us. Very well. We have been through difficult times before, and we have survived. In the end and finally, it all comes down to one simple question, doesn't it? Which is to come first: your will—or God's will?"

Another long silence, broken this time by a heavy sigh from Monsieur Vianney. "Oh, very well, my good woman!" He lifted his hands and dropped them again in a gesture of helplessness. "Jean-Marie shall go. You have won again."

A bright smile spread over Madame Vianney's rough features. "No, no", she said softly. "God has. In the end He always does!"

So Jean-Marie made ready to attend the Abbé Balley's private school at Ecully. In the beginning, however, there was trouble. Indeed, it looked for a time as if Jean-Marie would never go. Hearing that he wished to enter, Monsieur Balley sent word that he already had eleven students. He did not feel that he could handle one more.

Papa Vianney was delighted. He chortled to himself. "Good, good!" he said. "Perhaps, after all, we will not lose our hard-working Jean-Marie."

"We shall see!" his wife said in a tone of voice that wiped the smile straight off Monsieur Vianney's face.

Early the next morning Madame Vianney hitched the donkey to the cart and took off for Ecully. She returned at nightfall, all nods and smiles.

"Jean-Marie," she said, "Monsieur Balley wishes you to call on him in the morning."

"He has changed his mind? He has decided to take me into his school after all?"

"He has made no promises. However, he has agreed to talk to you tomorrow."

At noon the next day Jean-Marie stood in Monsieur Balley's combination office and bedroom at the rear of the presbytery.

The room was as bare as a prison cell, for Monsieur Balley was not a man for frills. Indeed, he was the despair of the Widow Bibost, his plump and cheery housekeeper. "The good priest allows himself no comforts whatsoever", she was forever complaining to the neighbors. "I prepare him the tastiest dishes, and what does he do? He sends them back to the kitchen and makes his meal on a crust of bread. Ah!" At this point the Widow Bibost always lowered her voice to a solemn whisper. "He is almost too good, the Monsieur Balley. Why, he lives as simply as Saint Anthony in the desert."

The Abbé Balley was known as the Curé of Ecully—curé because he was a pastor in charge of a parish, that is, of a cure of souls.

So Jean-Marie addressed him. "It was kind of the good curé", he said, "to ask me to call on him."

Monsieur Balley motioned him to one of the two chairs. He seated himself on the other.

The years had changed him, Jean-Marie could see. They had aged him greatly. They seemed to have shrunk him, too. "Though that", Jean-Marie reflected to himself, "may be simply because I have grown so.

He felt almost too big for the little room. He stared at his feet. Suddenly they seemed monstrous to him in their wooden shoes. He shifted his round shepherd's hat from one big hand to the other and wished he could hide the hat somewhere—and the hands too.

"So, Jean-Marie," Monsieur Balley said, "we meet again at last. You have changed somewhat since the night you hid me in the woods."

"One does, M'sieur."

"Yes, one does. People speak well of you, Jean-Marie."

"Oh, if you mean my mother, naturally, M'sieur. You know how mothers are. They always speak well of their sons."

"It is not only your mother who speaks well of you.

So does your Aunt Margaret, and that fine young farmer your sister Catherine has married. They say you are pious."

"I love God, M'sieur."

"That is part of it. Perhaps you love your neighbors too?"

"Of course, M'sieur. It would be silly to love God and not love His children too."

Monsieur Balley's mild eyes widened. He looked more closely at Jean-Marie. "So," he said, "you wish to join my school?"

"With all my heart."

"How old are you now?"

"I am twenty."

"Twenty, eh? The students I now have are mere boys. Would you not be uncomfortable studying with a group of boys? All of them are from five to ten years younger than yourself."

"Perhaps I will be uncomfortable, M'sieur. But what does it matter? One does not mind a few discomforts if it means pleasing God."

Monsieur Balley's eyes grew even wider now. Jean-Marie, of course, could not know what was going on in the little curé's mind. In truth, Monsieur Balley had not intended taking Jean-Marie into his school. He had meant to send him away with a few kind words. For the life of him, however, he could not resist Jean-Marie's saying that "one does not mind a few discomforts if it means pleasing God."

"Very well", he said, brushing a speck from his soutane. "You may join the school whenever you are ready."

Jean-Marie began his studies the next day. The classes were held around the big table in the presbytery dining room. As Monsieur Balley had said, the other scholars were mere boys. For a full-grown man, Jean-Marie was only of average height. Even so, he towered above the others. When he looked up from his book he found himself looking down on eleven dark, bowed heads.

Busy days! At his aunt's farmhouse on the fringe of Ecully he was up long before dawn and busy with his morning chores. Then off to Mass at the stone church. Breakfast at Monsieur Balley's was a roll and some weak beer. Then the classes began.

Latin was Jean-Marie's hard subject. It had taken him months to learn how to read his own language. But Latin! Latin was a horror to him.

Monsieur Balley was patience itself. "No, no, Jean-Marie," he would say, "you are mixing up the case endings again. Now listen and repeat after me. We will do the first declension of the singular of the word 'road'. After me, now.

And the little curé would proceed: "*Vi-a, vi-ae, vi-ae, vi-am, vi-a.*" Jean-Marie repeated the words perfectly. But later on, trying it himself, he mixed up the endings all over again.

Finally Monsieur Balley asked his brightest scholar,

twelve-year-old Mathias Loras, to tutor Jean-Marie in the afternoons. As a rule, they worked in the yard. Tramping the grass together, back and forth, the two of them made quite a sight for the neighbors.

Mathias was a regular little aristocrat, with a narrow, handsome face and dark eyes as sharp as tacks. Everything about him was always in order. Not so Jean-Marie. His clothes were rumpled and seemed to become more so with each step as he clumped along in his heavy shoes, hulking above his child-tutor.

One afternoon a light rain chased them indoors. They sat down on a sofa in the parlor, where some of the other boys were quietly studying their lessons.

"Now, Jean-Marie," Mathias said, "I'm going to say the sentence in our language once more. Then you give it to me in Latin. Now here is the sentence: 'Caesar was killed by Brutus.' What is the Latin now, please?"

"*Caesar*", Jean-Marie began falteringly, "*a Bruto interfect*— . . ." Oh, what was the proper ending for this part of the verb?

Little Mathias was on his feet. "Oh, really, Jean-Marie!" His youthful treble glided upward. "It is *interfectus*. I have told you a thousand times. And a thousand times you have got it wrong." In a sudden burst of temper he reached out and slapped Jean-Marie, sharply and hard, on his cheek.

All around the room the other boys looked up. There were surprise and eagerness in every pair of eyes—eagerness because, well, after all, scholars or no scholars, they sensed a scrap in the offing.

In this they were disappointed. Jean-Marie did not so much as frown. He dropped to his knees, cradling one of Mathias' small white hands in his own.

"Forgive me, Mathias", he said. "I know how I try your patience. I should have told you before we started. I am a dunce; I always have been. Why, once one of my own sisters told me as much, and she loves me dearly, too."

A profound silence succeeded these remarks. The other boys lowered their eyes. As for Mathias Loras, he looked first this way, then that, biting his lips. Then suddenly he leaned forward, hugging Jean-Marie and crying his eyes out. "Oh, Jean-Marie", he sobbed. "Thank you. You will never know what you have taught me this afternoon." And he flew out of the room.

Jean-Marie lumbered to his feet. "Taught *him*? What in the world could I teach him?" He did not realize that he was speaking out loud.

A boy sitting under one of the windows gave him his answer. "Humility, Jean-Marie", he said. "After all, there are other things than Latin in this world."

For three years Jean-Marie studied under the Abbé Balley. There were no more tantrums by Mathias Loras. On the contrary, the aristocratic little boy and the awkward farm youth became the closest and best of friends.

Toward the end of the first year Jean-Marie made a trip to the tomb of Saint François Régis, high on a mountain near the village of Louvesc, sixty miles away. Saint François Régis had worked many miracles for people. Perhaps, Jean-Marie reasoned, he would help him with his Latin.

He made the entire trip, back and forth, on foot and almost without money. He returned thinner than ever and deathly pale. Monsieur Balley took one look at him and uttered an exclamation of distress. "Jean-Marie, you must take to your bed for a few days", he said. "This trip has been too much for you."

Jean-Marie smiled. The next morning he was in his place again at the dining room table. Nor did his prayers to Saint François Régis go unanswered. All his life, Latin would be difficult for him, but little by little he did improve.

One morning he received distressing news. The Emperor Napoleon had lost some battles. He needed more soldiers. Previously young men studying for the priesthood had been exempt from service in the army. Now the exemption was canceled.

Jean-Marie gazed sadly at the slip of paper in his hand. It ordered him to report to the city of Lyon. There he would begin his training as a soldier in the Imperial Army.

6

JEAN-MARIE BECOMES AN OUTLAW

O N THE AFTERNOON of January 5, 1809, Jean-Marie trudged along the road leading south from the French city of Roanne. He was wearing the uniform of a private in the army of the Emperor Napoleon. A bulging knapsack was slung over his back.

Patches of snow lay on the ground, and the air was chill. Nonetheless, beads of sweat stood on Jean-Marie's forehead and occasionally washed into his eyes. He had been walking steadily for five hours. His face burned with prickly heat, and he felt tired and unwell.

Spying a snow-free ledge under a clump of trees, he climbed the bank to it and slipped off his knapsack. Reaching into the pocket of his coat, he took out the rosary Monsieur Balley had given him on his last day at the school in far-off Ecully. He had said the joyous mysteries when he put it back.

He felt the mossy earth with his hand—damp, but not too damp. Surely a few minutes' rest here would do him no harm. Making a pillow of his knapsack, he leaned it against a white boulder and stretched out.

An hour later a strong hand shook him awake. Looking up, Jean-Marie thought at first that a cloud had covered the sun. Then he saw that the cloud was a man wearing a uniform like his own—a tall, hulking young man with a laughing voice.

"You there," the laughing voice said, "you'll fill yourself with aches and pains sleeping on the cold ground."

Jean-Marie struggled to his feet. His legs and his shoulders felt as if clamps had been put on them and tightened. The man with the laughing voice was quite right.

The tall youth extended his hand. "People call me Guy", he said. "Guy of the Black Woods because I come from hereabouts. And you?"

"Vianney. Jean-Marie Baptiste Vianney." The "Bap-

tiste" was a new addition. It was the name of the patron saint Jean-Marie had selected at his confirmation
only a few years before. He dropped his eyes before
the other man's amused and curious gaze.

"You're a deserter, I suppose", Guy of the Black
Woods said. Then, seeing Jean-Marie's startled glance,
he added, "Don't be alarmed. I'm a deserter myself.
I've run away from the army, and I've no intention of
returning. There's a village here high in the woods. I
have friends there. They will be glad to hide me until
the wars are over." He stooped suddenly and picked
up Jean-Marie's knapsack. "Come along", he added.
"My friends can always find room for one more." He
strode off, climbing the slope in the direction of the
forest.

Jean-Marie had to run to catch up with him. "But,
M'sieur," he protested, "you are making a mistake."

"A mistake!" Guy halted. "You are not a deserter?"
He turned, facing Jean-Marie. "Why are you alone,
then? Where is your regiment?"

"My regiment . . ." Breathless, Jean-Marie had
trouble getting the words out. "My regiment left
Roanne a week ago. I was taken ill and put in a hospi-
tal. When I got out yesterday, I was told to catch up
with my regiment as best I could."

"And your regiment is going where?"

"To Spain."

"And it left Roanne a week ago, you say?"

"Yes, M'sieur."

"Then you will never catch up with it. Never. It is probably fifty miles or more from here already, and you are still a sick man. One can see that with half an eye. Besides—" A rumbling laugh shook Guy's big chest. "If I ever saw a man who was not cut out to be a soldier, you are he! Come along."

Again Guy of the Black Woods set out, this time at an even faster pace. Jean-Marie ran after him. "M'sieur!" he shouted. "Please, M'sieur. Give me my knapsack, and I will be on my way. I have no wish to be a deserter!"

"No wish!" Guy halted sharply. Once again he turned back. "You want to catch up with your regiment? You want to go to Spain? Whatever for? What is your regiment going to do in Spain?"

"I do not know, M'sieur." Jean-Marie hastened to join the other man. "I only know it has been ordered there", he said.

"But you have no idea what for?"

"How could I know? I am new in the army."

"When were you called in?"

"Eight weeks ago."

"And before that?"

"I was a student."

"A student?"

"I was studying for the priesthood."

"Ah!" A smile crept into the corners of Guy's eyes. With a shrug he threw Jean-Marie's knapsack on the ground. "Very well, then, take your knapsack. *But wait!*"

Jean-Marie, bending to pick up the knapsack, straightened up without it. He was startled by the sudden intensity in the other's voice.

Guy was staring at him in a strange way. "So, Jean-Marie," he said, "you were planning to give your life to God."

"That was my hope, M'sieur."

"Please don't call me 'M'sieur'. My name is Guy. We are not so formal in this part of the country."

"As you wish, Guy."

"And now," Guy was saying, "you want to go to Spain. You want to kill Spaniards for Napoleon. Is that your idea of giving your life to God?"

"I have no wish to kill anyone. But is it not one's duty to fight for his country?"

"For his own country, yes. But Napoleon is not asking you to fight for your country."

"For what, then?"

"For himself!" Guy chuckled. "Napoleon wants to conquer the world. That is all his wars amount to—that and nothing else. I do not believe in that. Live and let live is good for human beings. It is good for countries too. I myself cannot fight for Napoleon. He is a pig."

"*Ma Foi!*" Jean-Marie was shocked. "Should one say such things?"

"What else can one say? Oh, I admit Napoleon has done good things for France. He has made some good laws. But look at the other side of it. When he became our ruler he promised France peace. He has given us nothing but wars. When the wars started, he gave his word that he would not call to the army men who were studying to be priests—men like yourself. He has broken that promise."

Guy paused a second, frowning. "No!" he said. "It is not one's duty to fight for Napoleon. It is one's duty to refuse!" He pointed to the knapsack still lying at Jean-Marie's feet. "Well, you know the way back to the road. I am going the other way. Follow me or not as you think best." Turning away from Jean-Marie, he once again strode up the hill.

Jean-Marie stood motionless. Never in his life had he been more confused, more bewildered. Guy's words rang through his head: "Napoleon . . . pig . . . wants to conquer the world . . . has broken his promise . . . " With a sigh he stooped to pick up his knapsack. His lips moved. "Dear God," he said, "if it is the wrong thing I am doing, be merciful!"

He ran after Guy. The latter had stopped at the edge of the wood. When Jean-Marie reached him, Guy grabbed the knapsack and threw it over his shoulder.

"You are far from a well man yet, Jean-Marie," he said, "and we have a rough journey ahead of us."

All afternoon Jean-Marie and his new friend tramped up the mountain through the woods. They spent the night in the shack of an old shoemaker, a friend of Guy's. Dawn found them once more on their way, kicking through the drifts of a steadily falling snow. Toward noon they rounded the crest of the mountain.

Below, in the valley, Jean-Marie could see the huddled houses of a village half hidden by naked trees. Nearer, on the slope, lay the scattered buildings of some farms. "We have arrived!" In his excitement Guy of the Black Woods leaped into the air. His big hand fell heavily on Jean-Marie's shoulder. It was meant to be a friendly slap, but it sent Jean-Marie spinning.

Guy steadied him with a laugh. "The village of Noes!" He indicated the huddled houses far below. "There is our destination." His arm shifted in the direction of the nearest and largest farmhouse. "That is the home of my old friend Monsieur Fayot, the mayor of Noes. Monsieur Fayot's home is always open to those who refuse to aid Napoleon in his murderous wars."

Leaning his head into the snowstorm, Guy hurried on. "Come along!" he shouted. A second later they were in a large and smoky kitchen. Jean-Marie found himself being introduced to all sorts of people: a tall man with a curly beard, a pretty young woman, a half dozen children. So much noise, so much confusion! He was reminded of evenings in his boyhood—those evenings when the homeless refugees crowded into the kitchen of his parents' farmhouse in Dardilly.

And now he was a refugee himself, a deserter, an outlaw, and these shouting, laughing people were taking him into their home. In no time the long table in the center of the kitchen was lined with platters of steaming food. He was being propelled to a place alongside Guy.

At the far end of the table, Monsieur Fayot bowed his head in prayer. When he had finished grace, he got to his feet. He stood there a second, tugging at his beard and smiling, his eyes going from Guy to Jean-Marie and back again.

"Gentlemen," he said, "you are welcome here, welcome to stay as long as you like. Believe me, every man and woman and child in this village is on your side. I must tell you, however, that you will not be beyond danger among us. From time to time the soldiers of Napoleon come into the village, hunting for deserters. When that happens . . ."

Monsieur Fayot, puckering his lips, imitated the plaintive whistle of the whippoorwill. "That is our signal, gentlemen. Everyone in the village knows it. When you hear it, it means that soldiers have been sighted. It means hide, take cover, hope for the best. We will do all in our power to protect you."

Monsieur Fayot filled his wine glass and lifted it. He signaled to the others to do likewise. "And now, a toast!" he proclaimed. "A toast to the day Napoleon will tire of these wars and France once more is at peace with all nations."

Thus, in the mountain village of Noes, in the home of its genial mayor, Jean-Marie began his life as a deserter. There was room enough only for Guy in the mayor's home, so Jean-Marie was sent elsewhere. Late in the evening a small boy guided him across the moonlit fields to the home of the mayor's cousin, Madame Claudine.

There he was made comfortable in a corner of one of the barns. He was brought a chair and a table. One of Madame Claudine's little daughters brought him a handful of books, saying, "Because you are a student, M'sieur, and a candidate for the priesthood." The shy child was gone before Jean-Marie could express his thanks.

Madame Claudine was a widow, a cheerful and pleasant-faced young woman. She had four children in all, two girls and two boys. Her farm was big. There was no lack of work for Jean-Marie. He helped to look after the stock and made repairs on the house and outbuildings.

At supper in the low-beamed kitchen one evening, Madame Claudine said to him, "Jean-Marie, my children have had no schooling. Would you be good enough to give them lessons?"

Her request pleased Jean-Marie. It frightened him, too. He thought: I, who am the slowest of learners! What kind of a teacher will I make?

He made a good one, probably because he was such a slow learner. He was endlessly patient with the children. Soon all of them could read and write and do simple problems in arithmetic.

In the early spring there was a scare. Soldiers were sighted in the nearby woods. They were obviously hunting for deserters. Jean-Marie took to the fields, hiding in a shepherd's rough hut. Early the next morning one of Madame Claudine's boys came after him.

"It is all right now, M'sieur", he said. "The soldiers searched all the buildings, but they are gone now."

With the advance of spring the snows melted. The little road winding into Noes became passable. Another contingent of soldiers appeared at the farm. This time Jean-Marie did not even know of their presence until he returned from his work in the fields that evening, long after their departure.

A week later an early-morning storm gouged a hole in the roof of the barn where Jean-Marie slept. The minute the storm was over, he made haste to repair the damage. The day was hot and sunny after the downpour. Jean-Marie worked steadily, replacing the broken boards and covering them with straw thatching.

Occasionally he paused to watch Madame Claudine's boys playing nine-man morris in a nearby cedar grove. He could hear the church bells tolling in the village below. A cawing crow swooped close over the barn. His ears picked up the shrill plaint of a whippoorwill.

A whippoorwill? Jean-Marie was puzzled. Whippoorwills were rarely, if ever, seen in these parts. Then the sound came again, and he remembered. There was no whippoorwill! A quick glance told him that the sound came from one of the boys in the cedar grove. He could see the two of them standing back among the trees waving to attract his attention and pointing to the lane leading toward the farm.

He rose slightly from his crouched position on the roof—far enough to glance over the ridgepole. He could see them now, not the soldiers themselves, but the gleam of their bayonets as they approached the farmhouse.

He slid down the roof, dropping to earth. For a second, he hesitated, wondering as to the best place to hide. The safest course, he knew, would be to head for the fields. But if he tried that, there was the open slope to be traversed. The soldiers, marching across the higher ground now, would almost be certain to spot him.

He ducked into the barn and looked around. The hayloft, of course! He scrambled up the ladder. At the top, crouching beside the opening, his first impulse was to pull the ladder up after him. He decided otherwise on second thought. The soldiers might notice the absence of the ladder, in which case they would be sure to search the loft.

Besides, it was too late! He could hear the squish of their boots in the damp barnyard, their loud voices at the door.

He dived into a pile of hay in a dark corner, worming his body in as far as he could. The floorboards

shook beneath him, telling him that one—no, two—
of the soldiers had already ascended to the loft.

He could make out their words now. "You take that
side", a gravelly voice said. "I'll take this."

He made himself as still as his quivering muscles
would permit and held his breath.

It was hot in the hayloft, even hotter within the pile
of hay where Jean-Marie crouched in terror. To make
matters worse, the hay had fermented. Jean-Marie
held his breath as long as he could; when he did
breathe, the sour fumes of the hay all but gagged him.

He could hear the two soldiers moving methodi-
cally along the sides of the loft. He could hear the
thump, thump of their bayonets as they prodded the
thick hay.

His throat and nostrils burned. He fought back a
sneeze. A horrible picture formed in his mind—a picture of what would happen to Madame Claudine and
all of his kind friends in Noes if he were found! He
thought of Guy of the Black Woods, still hiding at the
mayor's house up the hill. Surely one of Madame
Claudine's children would think to run up the hill
with a warning for his fellow deserter.

He could hear the two soldiers muttering to one
another. They were drawing closer to the pile under
which he was hiding. He felt a sudden and stinging
pain in his left leg, the sickening smart of blood min-
gling with sweat.

One of the bayonets, he realized, had grazed his

skin. He held himself tight and prayed, somehow certain that the next thrust of the bayonet would find his heart and kill him. He heard a sound like the tearing of rough cloth. The bayonet slid by, missing his face by a hair.

Again he held himself tight and waited. He heard a rattling sound, then another. The ladder! Could it be that the soldiers were climbing down the ladder? Another rattle, the thud of boots on the floor below—then silence. They had gone!

The relief flooding through Jean-Marie was almost more painful than the previous tension. He forced himself to count slowly to five. Then, slowly, he lifted himself, shaking off the hay. The strain had told on him. His aching muscles refused to hold him erect. With a low groan he fell headlong onto the hay and lay there gasping for breath.

Minutes passed, a half hour, before one of Madame Claudine's boys came up the ladder and helped him to his feet.

"It is all right now, Jean-Marie", the lad told him. "The soldiers have left the village."

"And Guy of the Black Woods? Was he warned in time?"

"Indeed, yes. When the soldiers reached the mayor's house, Guy was hiding in the creek. He is quite safe."

Once more, during the long, hot summer, the soldiers came, but Jean-Marie was safely out of sight in a remote field.

The soldiers, to be sure, were not his only concern. His greatest concern was for his family in Dardilly.

Had his family been told that he was a deserter or that he was dead? If the military authorities thought him dead, then his family, knowing this, would grieve. If the authorities knew he was a deserter, then his family would be cruelly punished.

Napoleon's government was hard on the family of a man who deserted the army. A bailiff, a government official, was lodged in the home of the family. If the deserter did not turn himself in shortly, a second bailiff was lodged in his family's house, then a third, then a fourth. Soon there were so many bailiffs living in the house that the family had to sell some of its land to buy food for them. Guy of the Black Woods, coming down the hill to visit Jean-Marie, told him of one family that had lost all of its earthly possessions in this way.

At midsummer, Madame Claudine fell ill from overwork. Her doctor advised her to visit the baths in a resort town near the city of Lyon.

Jean-Marie was glad when Madame Claudine decided to make the trip, for the resort village was not far from his home in Dardilly. He gave Madame Claudine a hundred francs, all the money he had. "Please," he said to her, "pay a visit to my family. Tell them I am alive and safe; find out for me how they are getting along."

Madame Claudine returned in the fall. His family,

Jean-Marie learned, was all right. The government authorities had not bothered them. The family had assumed that Jean-Marie was dead, of course. They were overjoyed to hear that he was not. His mother had sent him his books—his Latin grammars. She had sent him, also, a letter.

"My dear son," she wrote, "you must study hard. Now, more than ever, I am certain that the dear Lord intended you to be a priest. Believe me when I say that all of us are well. We all send you our love. In this we are joined by your good friend Monsieur Balley, the Curé of Ecully."

Winter came early to Noes, once more blanketing the little village and the surrounding fields in white. With the spring of 1810 came exciting news. Napoleon had got an annulment of his marriage to the Empress Josephine and had married Marie Louise, daughter of Francis II, Emperor of Austria.

Many of the French people did not approve of the new marriage. In an effort to make himself more popular, Napoleon had issued what he called an amnesty. Under the terms of the amnesty, all deserters from the army were forgiven.

Guy of the Black Woods came down the hill to give Jean-Marie the news. "But, Guy," Jean-Marie said, "does this mean that . . . ?"

"It means", Guy broke in, "that you are free, Jean-Marie. You may return to your family in Dardilly!"

When Jean-Marie made ready to leave the next

morning, he found, to his surprise, that the towns-people were unhappy about his departure. Guy of the Black Woods came down the hill, along with the mayor and his family, to bid him good-bye.

"I am staying here," Guy told him, "and take my word for it, Jean-Marie, I shall miss you."

"We shall all miss you", the mayor said, tugging at his beard and batting his eyes to keep back the tears.

The village tailor arrived, bringing a soutane he had made for Jean-Marie. "Put it on", he insisted. "Put it on and wear it."

"Oh, no!" Jean-Marie shook his head vigorously. "It is not right for one who is not a priest to wear such a garment."

Madame Claudine added her plea to that of the tailor. "Please, Jean-Marie", she begged. "We may never see you after you become a priest. Let us see now what you are going to look like." So, to please his friends, Jean-Marie donned the soutane and wore it for an hour.

At the last minute an old and wrinkled woman hurried into the big kitchen. She pressed thirty francs into Jean-Marie's hands. Jean-Marie knew the old woman well. He knew that she was a widow and very poor. He tried hard to give the money back; the old woman would not take it.

"But, my good friend," he told her, "you must have starved yourself to save all this money."

"Not at all", the old woman replied. "I simply sold

my pig. But never mind", she added hastily, seeing Jean-Marie's look of concern. "I still have my billy goat."

It was noon and the sun was high and warm when Jean-Marie set out on the little road winding out of Noes. He walked rapidly. He had many miles to go, and he looked forward eagerly to seeing his mother again, his father, his brothers and sisters. He could hardly believe that only a few days hence he would once more shake the hand of Monsieur Balley.

At the bend in the road he turned and looked back. Noes lay peaceful under its trees. Above it, in a sun-baked clearing, he could see the farm of Madame Claudine; still farther up were the houses and out-buildings of the mayor. His eyes misted. He did not know it then, but he would never see the village of Noes again. He would never forget it, however—never in his life!

7

"HE WILL NEVER BECOME A PRIEST"

JEAN-MARIE sat in the parlor of the College of St. Irénée, a seminary for the training of priests, in the city of Lyon, France. He sat on the edge of the brocaded sofa, his thin legs stretched out before him. Arising at dawn that morning, he had made the journey from Ecully by foot.

His eyes traveled along the high, paneled walls, coming to rest on a painting of Cardinal Fesch, the bishop of the diocese. The cardinal, he remembered

Monsieur Balley telling him, was in Rome for the time being. In his absence the diocese was being administered by his chief assistant, a priest spoken of as the First Grand Vicar.

At the far end of the parlor a small door opened, and a young servant appeared. Jean-Marie looked up expectantly, but the servant shook his head.

"Not yet, M'sieur", he said. "Your turn will come soon."

The servant crossed the room into a large hallway. Shortly he returned, carrying a book. Smiling at Jean-Marie, he disappeared again beyond the small door.

Jean-Marie stared at the window, bright with the sun of a spring morning. Almost four years had passed since his departure from Noes. Four eventful years! His mother had died a few weeks after his return home. He had always known that he would miss her; he had never realized how much until she was gone.

With more vigor than ever, he had plunged into his studies with Monsieur Balley at Ecully. In time, Monsieur Balley had sent him on to a higher seminary. There he had struggled through his courses somehow; but at the highest seminary of all, his weakness in Latin had defeated him. Six months after his entrance he had been told to return to Ecully for further training.

How he and Monsieur Balley had worked then! How many nights they had sat up, practically until dawn, reading Latin together. And now . . . !

In his nervousness Jean-Marie gripped the seat of the sofa with his hands. He stared at the little door. In the office beyond it sat the priests who would give him his final oral examination. If he passed the examination, he would become a priest. If not . . . !

Jean-Marie sighed. He was certain he knew the answers to any questions the examining priests might ask him. Even so, he was frightened. The questions would be asked in Latin, and suppose he did not quite understand the words? No one could answer a question if he did not understand the language in which it was put.

The little door had opened again. This time the servant nodded to Jean-Marie and indicated that he was to enter the office.

There were half a dozen of the clergy in the other room. Jean-Marie recognized the tall, elderly priest who bore the honored title of "Canon". Sitting behind the big desk, Canon Bochard smiled and gave Jean-Marie a friendly nod. He introduced him to the other priests and indicated he was to sit in a chair in front of the desk.

"And now, Jean-Marie," he said, "since our examination of the other candidates has taken more time than we expected, we will start at once. Is that all right with you?"

"Yes, my lord." Only three words, but Jean-Marie had trouble saying them. His mouth was parched, and his hands, clutching at his hat, were shaking.

"Now, then." Canon Bochard smiled again at Jean-Marie. "I understand that Latin is difficult for you, so I will ask my questions slowly. Are you quite ready, Jean-Marie?"

"Yes, my lord."

With great slowness then, Canon Bochard put his first question.

"*An teneamur*", he began, "*dilligere nostros inimicos?*"

Poor Jean-Marie! The canon had asked him a very simple question. "Are we obliged", he had inquired, "to love our enemies?" Had the canon asked him this question in French, Jean-Marie could have answered it at once and correctly. He would simply have said, "Of course we must love our enemies. Christ has ordered us to love everyone." After that, the canon would have gone on to the next question.

But Jean-Marie did not understand the words. In his nervousness it was as if all the Latin Monsieur Balley had pounded into his head had simply poured out of it. It was as if he had never learned the declension of a single Latin noun or conjugated a single verb.

He stared blankly at Canon Bochard. His hands shook so, that the hat fell from his lap. Perspiring with embarrassment, he picked it up.

Some of the priests looked at each other with raised eyebrows. Not so Canon Bochard. He gave Jean-Marie another of his friendly smiles.

"You are very nervous", he said. "Shall I repeat the question?"

"Please, my lord."

Again then: "*An teneamur dilligere nostros inimicos?*"

Jean-Marie stared beyond the canon to the window behind him.

"*An teneamur . . . ?*" That meant—oh, what did it mean? What did any of it mean? His eyes withdrew from the window and found the floor. He was seized with a sudden desire to leap to his feet and run from the room, to keep on running as far as his breath allowed.

Canon Bochard had arisen. He came around the desk, taking Jean-Marie's hands and pulling him to his feet.

"Enough for today, Jean-Marie", he said gently. "I have only good reports of you from Monsieur Balley. I am confident you are worthy to be a priest, but of course a priest must know Latin. Return to Monsieur Balley, young man. Study with him some more, and come back to us another day."

"You mean, my lord, I may take the examination again?"

"You may, young man. Whenever you feel you are ready for it."

Jean-Marie could hardly have been happier had he passed the examination. This was not the end, then, after all! He was to have another chance. His spirits soared. They fell, however, as one of the other priests spoke to the man beside him. He spoke in Latin, but, strangely enough, Jean-Marie understood him perfectly.

"What a country bumpkin this one is", the young priest said. "He will never become a priest."

Canon Bochard heard him, too. He frowned as he moved his hand in blessing over Jean-Marie, who had dropped to his knees. Regaining his feet, Jean-Marie tried to speak, but no words came. Turning from the canon, his eyes hot with tears, he hurried out of the room.

"He will never become a priest!"

All the way back to Ecully, those words—the only words in Latin he had been able to understand during his examination—rang in Jean-Marie's ears. Walking steadily and fast, he arrived in Ecully at nightfall.

The Abbé Balley was reading in his combination study and bedroom. He leaped up as Jean-Marie entered and gave the young man a searching look. He did not have to ask how he had made out. No one in the world knew Jean-Marie better, or loved him more, than the Curé of Ecully. One look at Jean-Marie's face told him what had happened.

"Ah!" he said. "I am sorry!"

"I am sorry, too, M'sieur", Jean-Marie said. His nervousness had left him. He spoke calmly and in a clear voice. "I am sorry because of all the time you have devoted to teaching me."

"That's not important, Jean-Marie. We shall try again and . . ."

Jean-Marie did not let the old man finish. "But your efforts shall not go to waste, M'sieur", he said.

"Tomorrow I shall return to Lyon. I shall offer my services as a lay brother to some order there."

"You will do nothing of the sort!" The Curé of EculⓁy was the mildest of men. At this moment, however, his words were thunder. "You will do nothing of the sort!" he repeated, stepping closer to Jean-Marie. "It is not God's will that you be a lay brother. I know, as I know the sun will rise tomorrow, that He means for you to serve Him on His altar. Jean-Marie, do you remember the priest who heard your first confession?"

"M'sieur Groboz? Of course I remember him. Why do you ask?"

"Because M'sieur Groboz now holds a position of importance in the church in Lyon. I will see him tomorrow. I am certain that he will be able to suggest something."

Early the next morning Monsieur Bailey set out for Lyon. When he returned that evening he was smiling and chirping to himself. Jean-Marie was waiting in the presbytery parlor. "Well, M'sieur Curé?" he inquired.

"Be of good cheer, Jean-Marie!" The Abbé Balley's voice bubbled. "Tomorrow you and I have an appointment with M'sieur Courbon, the First Grand Vicar himself!"

Together, the next day, the priest and the awkward young man walked to Lyon. Together they presented themselves at the bishop's palace and were ushered into a large parlor dark with heavy draperies.

"Be of good cheer, Jean-Marie!" Monsieur Balley kept saying. "This is a great day in your life."

Indeed it was one of the greatest. Jean-Marie felt it was going to be when Monsieur Courbon, the First Grand Vicar, entered the room. The Grand Vicar was old and thin and homely, but there was a shine about him, a glow.

His voice was gruff, his manner brusque. "There, there!" he said after the priest and the young man had received his blessing. "Take chairs, take chairs." He seated himself and glared at Jean-Marie. "Son," he said, "you wish to be a priest?"

"Yes, my lord."

"Well, heaven knows France needs them. Far too many churches are still empty." He stared even harder at Jean-Marie. "But you have trouble with the Latin, they tell me."

"I am a poor learner, my lord."

"Well, well! Latin is important, but it is not everything. As a matter of fact . . ." The Grand Vicar leaned toward Jean-Marie and lowered his voice. "They tell me", he said, "that the Devil speaks Latin beautifully!"

"I did not know that, my lord. If it is true, I can only say that I envy him."

"You do, eh?" A dry chuckle from the Grand Vicar. He leaned toward Jean-Marie. "And you failed your oral examination?"

"Yes, my lord."

"Very well, then. I shall give you another examination. I shall ask you some questions. On second thought I will not put my questions to you. I will put them to Monsieur Balley."

He turned abruptly to the Curé of Ecully. "Now heed me, M'sieur", he went on. "I have only three questions, and I want short answers. Mind you, now, I want no ifs and ands, no whereases and wherefores, no sermons or dissertations. You understand me, M'sieur?"

"I will do the best I can", Monsieur Balley said.

"Very well, then. Question one: Does Jean-Marie truly have the faith?"

"Yes, my lord."

"Is he truly devoted to the Blessed Virgin Mary?"

"Yes, my lord."

"Does he know his Rosary?"

"Yes, my lord."

The Grand Vicar made a rumbling sound in his throat. He turned again to Jean-Marie. "Very well, then", he said. "Since the answer to all of my questions is yes, I hereby call you, Jean-Marie Baptiste Vianney, to the priesthood. It is obvious that you are a young man of great piety." For the first time the Grand Vicar's voice grew soft. "God", he finished, "will do the rest!"

On the following August 13, 1815—slightly less than a month after Napoleon's final defeat by the British at the Belgian town of Waterloo—Jean-Marie

Baptiste Vianney was at long last ordained. He was twenty-nine years old, thin, angular, square-faced. His feet still turned out. His smile was as shy and as crooked as ever. He still had the rough look and the clumsy gait of a French farm boy.

The ceremony took place in the chapel of the Grand Seminaire in the city of Grenoble. The next day was the Vigil of the Assumption. Jean-Marie celebrated his first Mass, after which he returned to Ecully, for to his joy he had been named assistant to the Abbé Balley.

In calling Jean-Marie to the altar, the First Grand Vicar had placed a limit on his activities. It was not only in Latin that Jean-Marie was weak. He had difficulty in learning the finer points of religion. For this reason he was ordered to study hard for one more year, during which he was not permitted to hear confessions. When the year was up, his first penitent was the Abbé Balley himself.

For three years, busy and content, Jean-Marie labored in Ecully. Then one winter evening the kind and saintly Abbé Balley died in his sleep.

After the funeral, Jean-Marie stood in his old friend's combination study and bedroom. The Abbé Balley had left Jean-Marie his few personal possessions—some books, a wooden rosary, a small, cracked mirror. For some seconds Jean-Marie stood staring sadly at these objects. Then, with a sigh, he hurried from the room and into the kitchen, where Madame

Bibost, the presbytery housekeeper, was preparing the noon meal.

"Madame," he said, entering the long sunlit room, "did the Abbé Balley ever have a picture made of himself?"

"A picture!" Turning from the fire, the Widow Bibost gave Jean-Marie a look as reproachful as her good-natured features would permit. "Surely you don't need a picture to remember our dear, dead friend."

"Of course not. Still," and Jean-Marie waved his big hands in a vague gesture, "it would be nice to have a picture of him to look at now and again."

"I am afraid there is no picture. However, I'll look. I'll search the house."

All day the Widow Bibost searched. That evening she was forced to report that there was no picture of the late Abbé Balley. "I'm sorry, M'sieur Curé", she said.

Jean-Marie frowned. "As I have told you before, Madame," he said, "you must not address me as 'M'sieur Curé.' I am not the pastor here; I am still only the assistant."

"But you have done so well here, and the people love you so. Surely, now that the abbé is dead, you will become the pastor in his place."

"That is for the Church to decide. I can only go on as I am and await orders."

He did not have to wait long. A few days later he

was summoned to Lyon. Once again he stood in the presence of Monsieur Courbon, the First Grand Vicar.

The aging vicar fixed Jean-Marie with his sharp eyes. "Well, Jean-Marie," he said, "I have much to tell you. In the first place I am sending another priest to take the place of the Abbé Balley in Ecully. You, however, are to have a pastorate of your own. I am sending you to the village of Ars some twenty-five miles to the north and east of us here."

The vicar paused, looking hard at Jean-Marie. "Do you know the village of Ars?" he inquired.

"No, my lord. I have never so much as heard of it."

"Well, it is a small place—some two hundred souls, more or less. It stands on the Fontblin River, on a large plateau known as the Dombes. There is a small church and a small stone presbytery. The church is seven hundred years old. I understand that it is in bad repair. During the revolutionary days it was used as a social club."

"And the people of Ars, my lord? What sort are they?"

"What sort indeed!" The vicar uttered his dry chuckle. "I will be frank with you, Jean-Marie. There is very little love of God in Ars. Your job will be to put some in it."

Back in Ecully, Jean-Marie hired a cart to transport his bed and the books Monsieur Balley had left him. He packed the rest of his belongings in his army knapsack. Among them he placed Monsieur Balley's wooden rosary and his small, cracked mirror.

At the last minute the Widow Bibost announced her intention of traveling with him. "But, Madame," Jean-Marie objected, "the new priest will be here tomorrow. He will need your services."

"He can spare me for a week or so. I will stay only long enough to see that you are comfortably settled in your new home."

"But I can settle myself."

"Oh, no, you can't!" The Widow Bibost's laugh rang through the presbytery kitchen. "I hear it is cold and damp in Ars. If you go by yourself, I know exactly what will happen."

Madame Bibost laughed more loudly than before. "You will forget to build a fire in the presbytery and come down with a cold in two days' time", she went on cheerfully. "The cold will go into grippe, the grippe into pneumonia. You will be dead and gone—God forbid!—before you have prepared your first Sunday sermon. Oh, no, M'sieur Curé!" The plump widow laughed again. "For I can call you M'sieur Curé now", she added. "I shall go along with you to Ars."

In truth, Jean-Marie was glad of the cheerful woman's company. They set out on foot, taking turns guiding the donkey Jean-Marie had purchased to pull his cart.

It was a mild, cloudy February day. Noon found them crossing the bridge over the Saône River at the city of Villefranche. East of the river the landscape changed. The road was no longer a tunnel through the heavy forest. They had reached the Dombes plateau, a vast, rolling area, open except for an occasional clump of birch and a scattering of steel-colored lakes. The fields, stretching endlessly ahead, had a grim and undressed look.

Night came and with it a light fog. Jean-Marie took a lantern from the cart and lighted it. Even so, they missed a fork in the road and would have wandered on aimlessly for miles had they not encountered two young shepherds driving their flocks.

The shepherds had never heard of Ars, but they were certain it was not on the road which they were traveling. On their advice Jean-Marie and the widow returned to the fork and tried the other road.

An hour later, picking their way down a rocky hill, they spotted in the gloom the crouching buildings of the village of Ars. The fog lifted as they crossed the little bridge over the Fontblin. The pale light of a winter moon revealed two rows of clay houses, their low, thatched roofs overhanging a single rutted road.

There were almost no windows on the street side. The walls of the houses stared at them like blind faces as they hurried by. At the end of the street was an open space, ragged with dead weeds. On the far side, perched on a rise of ground, stood the church. The presbytery, a somewhat larger building, stood on the gospel side, a cemetery on the other.

At his first glimpse of the church, with its high wooden steeple, Jean-Marie fell to his knees. His lips moved in prayer—a prayer of thanks that God had seen fit to place in his hands the spiritual care of this meanest of villages.

It was some time before Jean-Marie rose and he and the widow moved on. At the church steps they parted. Taking the reins of the donkey, Madame Bibost went at once to the presbytery. Jean-Marie hurried into the church.

At the door he paused, holding his lantern over his head. It was a high, narrow room, consisting of a single nave and a deep, half-moon sanctuary. As the First Grand Vicar had told him, it was badly in need of repairs. The yellow glow of the lantern showed huge cracks in the walls. In sections the plaster had crumbled away, exposing the wooden laths beneath.

Hurrying forward, Jean-Marie knelt at the foot of the altar. Then and there he dedicated his first parish to the Blessed Mother of God and asked her guidance in the days ahead. Regaining his feet, he went into the sacristy. It too was unswept and shabby. A door, he found, opened on a stone path leading through a hawthorn hedge to the rear stoop of the presbytery.

The Widow Bibost was a fast worker. Already she had removed Jean-Marie's bed from the cart and set it up in the largest of the three bedrooms on the second floor. She had prepared another room for herself at the rear of the house. A fire burned on every hearth. A pot of food simmered over the kitchen flames.

Jean-Marie tramped through the two rooms of the ground floor and up the stone steps to the floor above. After seeing the church, he had expected the presbytery also to be in bad shape. On the contrary, it was clean as a pin. Elaborate furniture crowded every room.

"Are not the furnishings grand?" the Widow Bibost called to him as he returned to the warm kitchen.

"Too grand!" said the new Curé of Ars, shaking his head.

"But, M'sieur, how can the home of a man of God ever be too grandly furnished?"

"Too grand", Jean-Marie repeated firmly. "The presbytery is too grand, and the church is not grand enough." He seated himself before the plate of food Madame Bibost had placed on the big kitchen table. "However, we will change all that in short order."

After the meal, Jean-Marie left the widow to tidy the kitchen and retired to the big room she had made ready for him on the second floor. He smiled to himself, examining the bed. The Widow Bibost had piled it high with sheets and blankets and a mammoth comforter. Stripping it rapidly, Jean-Marie removed the mattress. Then he lay two of the blankets, the thinnest two, over the wooden frame. Thus he had always slept at Ecully, and he had no intention of making himself any more comfortable here.

Putting out his lamp, he knelt to say his final prayers. As he was about to get into bed, a sudden thought brought a smile to his lips. Relighting the lamp, he went to the dresser where Madame Bibost had deposited his old army knapsack. Digging into it, he brought out the mirror—the small, cracked mirror that had belonged to the Abbé Balley.

He placed it on the mantle and stood for a minute smiling at it fondly. As he had told the Widow Bibost, he would like to have had a picture of the abbé to look at now and again. Lacking that, he would make do with this mirror that over the years had so often reflected the beloved face of his dead friend.

8

A PASTOR FOR ARS

I T WAS EARLY in February 1818 that Jean-Marie
arrived in the village of Ars. When he retired the
first night, he had no way of knowing, of course, what
lay ahead. Could he have peered into his own future,
he would have been amazed, possibly frightened. His
lifework had begun. For forty-one years, all the remaining years of his life, Ars would be his pastorate.
During those years—thanks to him—his mean little

village would become one of the most famous places in France, indeed, in all Europe.

Jean-Marie never allowed himself more than three or four hours of sleep. That first night in Ars he remained in bed less than two. He was up with the dawn. The Widow Bibost still slept. Downstairs, in the big kitchen, Jean-Marie piled pine logs on the hearth and got the fire going for her.

Leaving the house by the front door, he stood for a few minutes on the stone steps. In the watery, winter-morning light, the single street of the village looked more desolate than before. The houses, all joined to one another, presented two long walls, blank except for windowless doors and an occasional storefront. Every house was built of the same yellowish clay under the same roughly thatched roof.

Jean-Marie walked to the rear of the presbytery. The village, he saw, ended at this point. Beyond lay a spreading apple orchard. Beyond that there were rocky fields, bare save for an occasional walnut tree or lank elm.

He entered the church by way of the sacristy. He could see the long, narrow nave more clearly now. It looked frightful in the morning light, with its high, slit windows and rotting woodwork. He said his prayers and went into the vestibule. Finding the bell rope, he gave it a hard pull.

At first the bells, high in the wooden steeple, sounded uncertain and cracked, as though hoarse from disuse. A few more tugs and they were ringing out loud and clear.

In the dusty sacristy he vested slowly, saying more prayers. He entered the sanctuary to say his first Mass in Ars.

A glance told him that his congregation was small—a handful of old women. He could hear them whispering among themselves as he approached the altar. All through the opening prayers the whispers continued. He thought of the words the First Grand Vicar had spoken: "There is very little love of God in Ars." Obviously it was not the love of God that had brought these old women to church. Curiosity had brought them. They merely wished to see what their new pastor looked like.

"Very well," Jean-Marie murmured to himself as he re-entered the sacristy at the end of the Mass, "after breakfast I will give them a closer look. At the same time I will get a closer look at them."

Back in the big presbytery kitchen he ate his breakfast—a cup of milk. Loudly the Widow Bibost scolded him. "You listen to me now, M'sieur Curé", she shouted. "It was all right for you to eat next to nothing in Ecully. Your duties were not quite so difficult. But here you are the curé. You have great responsibilities. I cannot advise you too strongly to begin each day with a hearty breakfast."

Jean-Marie merely smiled and nodded and drank his milk, after which he departed, leaving the Widow

Bibost to consume the hot rolls and steaming coffee she had prepared for him.

He spent the day going up and down the street and out along the country lanes, calling on his people. Most of them, he found, were farmers like himself. He knew how to talk to such people. What were their crops, he asked them. How large were their flocks? In what condition were their plows?

He found the people faultlessly friendly. Everywhere he went he was offered food and drink, which he refused. He was offered a chair, which he usually refused, preferring to stand. Yes—they were friendly people, likeable, good-natured.

But, as he had been warned, they were not much interested in religion.

"It's like this, M'sieur Curé", an old man told him. "When Napoleon opened the churches, it was some time before a priest was sent to this little town. Finally they did send an old man. Alas! He was sick with the consumption when he arrived. Well, in this damp climate you can imagine how it was. Twenty-three days— only twenty-three—he lingered among us, and then!" The old man snapped his fingers. "Poof! He was gone!"

"God rest his soul", Jean-Marie added, blessing himself.

The old man tardily followed suit. "Ah, yes", he said, glancing upward with a look half pious and half amused. "No doubt the Good Lord will do that for him."

For three days Jean-Marie visited among his new parishioners. In the evenings, with the Widow Bibost's assistance, he worked in the church cleaning it up.

By the end of the third day the church was free of dust and cobwebs. By that time too, Jean-Marie knew a great deal about the village of Ars.

He knew that, small as it was, it had no fewer than four bars with dance halls attached. Cabarets, the people called them. He knew that in the evenings practically all of the men of the area, and many of the younger women, could be found in these cabarets.

Sunday in Ars, he learned, was regarded as simply another weekday. The men and women either worked in the fields or sang and danced in the cabarets.

He knew that lying was common among them; so were stealing and gossip. He knew that they neglected their children. The youngsters ran wild in the streets and fields. They had no manners, no respect for their elders or for each other. Only a handful of them had been baptized. Three-fourths of the older ones had never been confirmed. None had had so much as one lesson in the catechism.

In short, the people of Ars had quite forgotten God.

That is, most of them had. He did find, out in the countryside, four genuinely religious families. And on Saturday he made a happy discovery. Religion had a good friend, he learned, in Mademoiselle des Garets, the aging mistress of the gloomy chateau standing in a thick pine forest on the high bank across the river. It was Mademoiselle des Garets, he was told, who had supplied the presbytery with its elegant furniture.

Returning to the presbytery that evening, Jean-Marie announced, "Madame Bibost, we will not work in the church tonight. I have discovered that our furniture is the gift of the mistress of the chateau. We will load it on the cart this evening and return it to her."

"M'sieur Curé!" Madame Bibost turned to him with the saddest look he had ever seen in her usually cheerful eyes. "You don't really mean to give up all this fine furniture. Why should you?"

"Because, Madame, I am a mere man and have no right to such grandeur. Consider, Madame!" He pointed in the direction of the church. "Consider the squalor *He* is living in next door!"

"Oh, that can be changed. The church can be beautified."

"You can be sure it will be in due time. Meanwhile, I have no intention of keeping these things here. Come! We will begin with the heavier pieces in the living room."

It took them two hours to load the cart. In vain Madame Bibost pleaded and wailed and protested. In the end she did win a point. She persuaded the Curé to keep a few rush-bottomed chairs, one table, and some of the kitchen utensils.

They started down the street in pitch darkness,

walking alongside the donkey. The loose planks of the little bridge rattled as they crossed the river.

It was a chill, foggy night. A small boy, riding a lame horse, came up from behind and reined his mount to a walk. "Is it to the chateau you are going, M'sieur Curé?" he called,

"Yes, lad, to the chateau."

"Good, I work there, M'sieur. I will tell the mistress you are coming."

The boy clattered off. They could hear the echo of his horse's hoofs, diminishing gradually into silence.

It was all uphill after they left the bridge. A winding drive, flanked by pines, brought them to the front door of the chateau.

Jean-Marie pulled the bell knob. Almost at once a manservant, carrying a candelabra, opened the door. He was old and bent and apparently nearsighted. For some seconds he leaned toward them, peering. Then, "Ah, it is the Curé. Come in, M'sieur. Mademoiselle has been told that you were arriving."

The Widow Bibost did not go in. She waited outside, holding the donkey's reins and grumbling to herself.

Jean-Marie followed the servant across a dark, cavernous hall and through what appeared to be a small music room. The servant threw open a double door, and Jean-Marie stepped into a long, ornate parlor. At the far end a high fire danced on the mammoth grate.

Mademoiselle des Garets was not alone. As Jean-Marie entered, a tall, portly man arose from his chair near the fire. He came forward, his hand outstretched.

"M'sieur Curé," he said, "I have looked forward to meeting you. I am M'sieur Mandy, the mayor."

"Ah, yes. I have called at your home, M'sieur Mandy."

"So my wife and my children have told me. I am sorry I was not there. But now Mademoiselle des Garets is eager to meet you."

The mistress of the chateau had already risen from her chair. For some time she rested her smaller hand in his. Jean-Marie liked her at once. At sixty-four, Mademoiselle des Garets—more commonly known as the Mademoiselle of Ars—was a tall, strong-looking woman with handsome features and dark, heavily lidded eyes.

"M'sieur Curé," she said, "my boy tells me that you are returning the furniture. He also tells me that you brought very little of your own. I hope you are not depriving yourself."

"I have enough for my needs, Mademoiselle. I hope my returning yours does not offend."

"Of course not. Only—only I do want to do something for you. Are you sure there is nothing you need?"

"Nothing." Jean-Marie would have left it at that, only suddenly a thought struck him. He went on hastily. "I mean, Mademoiselle, that I need nothing for the presbytery. Now for the church—that is another matter."

"The church?"

"Have you been inside the church lately?"

"No, M'sieur Curé. I have been away for months. I returned only this afternoon."

"When you come to Mass in the morning, observe closely. You will agree with me, I'm sure. The church needs many repairs."

"What kind of repairs?"

"The walls, the steeple."

"The steeple?"

"Yes, Mademoiselle. The wooden steeple cannot last much longer. Besides, a building like that—it should have a steeple made of brick or stone."

"And how much would your repairs cost?"

Jean-Marie had a sum of money in mind. It was a large sum. He mentioned a somewhat smaller one. Immediately he wished he had mentioned the larger amount, for Mademoiselle des Garets promptly nodded.

"Have the repairs made," she said, "and send the bill to me. Now, is there anything else?"

"Yes, Mademoiselle. The vestments. Those I found in the sacristy are torn and soiled. I realize God pays little or no attention to such matters. Still, when one stands before Him, it is only respect to be well dressed."

Mademoiselle was nodding again. "Get the vestments, M'sieur Curé," she said. "I will pay for those too."

Jean-Marie left the chateau feeling extremely happy. He would have felt less so had he heard the conversation following his departure. He hated and feared praise of himself, and Mademoiselle's words were just that.

"M'sieur Mayor," she said, turning to her remaining guest as Jean-Marie left the room, "do you see what I see in that awkward little man?"

"What do you see, Mademoiselle?"

"A saint, M'sieur Mayor." The Mademoiselle of Ars lowered her heavy eyelids and sighed deeply. "A living saint!"

Returning to the presbytery with the Widow Bibost, Jean-Marie went at once to his room. It was late, but he had many things to do before retiring.

His first act was to strip from the wooden frame of his bed one of its thin blankets. Sometime the next day he would give it to one of the villagers, an old man who was sick and without money. He had already given the old man his mattress and the rest of his bedding.

During the week he had decided that it would take a long time to bring the citizens of Ars back to God. Meanwhile, someone must do penance for their sins. Very well, that someone would be he.

Kneeling, he offered up a prayer. "Dear God," he prayed, "I will make every sacrifice I can. I will eat less, sleep less, turn my back on every comfort. I implore you to accept my sacrifices not only as penance for my own sins, but for those of my parishioners too. Forgive them, Lord, for they know not what they do."

Rising, he went to the little table—one of the pieces of furniture the Widow Bibost had persuaded him to keep.

Scattered over the table were sheets of paper on which he had written the sermon he planned to deliver in the morning. He had worked on it off and on all week. It would be his first sermon in Ars. He wanted it to be a good one.

Reading it over, he sighed to himself. He remembered sermons he had heard at the seminary in Lyon. How beautifully they had been written; how eloquently they had been delivered. Well, God had given him no talents as a writer or a speaker. He could only do his best.

He read the sermon over again, changing a phrase here, another there. Then, for two hours, he paced the floor, memorizing every word.

As he expected, there were not many people at his first Sunday Mass. Entering the sanctuary, preceded by a small boy, he saw that the little room was less than half filled. Again the congregation consisted mostly of old women; and again, as he approached the altar, they whispered among themselves.

They quieted as the Mass proceeded. The church was quite still when the time came for the sermon.

He mounted the pulpit steps with quaking knees and stood a while in silence, clutching the wooden railing. For a dreadful second he was afraid he would never find his voice.

But it came. He heard himself faltering out the words he had so painstakingly written down and memorized. He faltered on. Once, during a long pause, he heard an ugly sound. He was not quite certain about it, but he could have sworn that it was suppressed laughter, that someone at the back of the church was laughing at him!

He continued. In his mind's eye he could see the white sheets of paper on which he had written his sermon.

Then suddenly the thing happened—the terrible thing he had feared. The words disappeared!

In panic he searched his mind only to find it blank. His eyes traveled over the grim walls. Without reason, without logic, he somehow expected to find the missing words there. But they were not. He saw only the dirty cracks, the gaping wood where the plaster had crumbled away.

He lowered his head, suffering an agony beyond anything he had ever endured before. A fearful thought came to him, a thought he would be ashamed of for the rest of his life—the thought that God had surely played some horrible joke in lifting such an unworthy man as himself to the priesthood.

Again he searched his mind, and again. It was no use. The rest of the sermon—the words he had tried so hard to memorize—was gone, gone!

There was only one thing he could do. Tremblingly he descended from the pulpit and returned to the altar. Slowly he began the Creed.

It was then that he heard the sound again. This time there was no doubt about it. People were tittering! They were laughing at him! He went on doggedly. Doggedly he completed his Mass. In the sacristy, afterward, he dismissed the altar boy with a despairing gesture and sat down on the room's only chair. An hour later Madame Bibost found him, still sitting there, and insisted on his coming to the presbytery for his breakfast, his cup of milk.

He spent his second week in Ars much as he had spent the first. On Monday he rounded up some workmen and got the church repairs under way. Midway in the week the Widow Bibost left for Ecully, having arranged for a younger woman to come in by day and keep the presbytery tidy.

Jean-Marie walked as far as the bridge with her. He smiled and nodded as Madame Bibost uttered her parting words of advice. "Now, M'sieur Curé," she said, "I can only hope you will soon mend your ways. You cannot expect to keep well on some milk and a few boiled potatoes a day. You must eat more, sleep more, and keep yourself warm."

She departed. Jean-Marie stood at the bridge, watching until her round, bouncy figure disappeared from view.

On Sunday he took no chances. Before Mass he laid

the white sheets of paper on the pulpit stand. When the time came he read his sermon.

There were no titters when he finished. But then, there were very few people to titter—even fewer than on the Sunday before. Mademoiselle des Garets was there, of course, accompanied as always by her bent, old manservant. The mayor and his family were there, the four truly religious families from out in the country, a few old women, and no more.

On the following Sunday, Jean-Marie again read his sermon. He did the same on the Sunday after that. On his fifth Sunday in Ars, however, he decided to try once more to give the sermon without the help of his white sheets of paper.

He mounted the pulpit grimly. He grasped the wooden railing with sweating hands and began. He faltered out a few sentences, a few more—and then, blankness! Just as on his first Sunday, the rest of his sermon simply disappeared! He had labored so hard on this one, too. Night after night, all week long, he had paced his room, memorizing the words. And now they were gone. All gone!

He bowed his head, overcome with shame. He braced himself against the titters he was sure would soon come from the people before him.

But no titters came. Instead, a strange thing happened, a thing that would be talked about in the village of Ars for many years to come.

In a high, resounding voice Jean-Marie began

speaking. He did not speak the words he had written down on his white sheets of paper. Other words came to him, he knew not from where. He spoke them, he knew not how. For a time he scarcely heard what he was saying. Then it came to him that he had said some of these words before.

He remembered how, as a boy, he and his sister Gothon had made clay shrines in the fields for his little statue of the Virgin. He remembered how they had staged processions, carrying the Blessed Mother and singing to her. He remembered how some of the neighbors' boys, one day, had come and teased them. He remembered giving the boys some of his own bread, thus bribing them to take part in the procession. He remembered gathering his playmates around him after the procession and giving them a sermon, imitating the words and gestures of his beloved Monsieur Balley.

And now—now he was saying the same words, or, at any rate, words very like them. And he was crying. He could feel the hot tears on his cheeks. He closed his eyes as tightly as he could and spoke on.

"Oh, my friends," he said, "I have not been long in Ars, but I have observed you closely. I see how you live. When Sunday comes, you go to the fields or to the cabarets. Back and forth you go in front of the church, but many of you do not stop or think to pay a visit to God.

"My friends, I know what you are thinking, too.

You are thinking, 'Of course, M'sieur Curé is a priest. Of course, he disapproves of the way we live.'

"No, my friends. No, no, no. It is not disapproval I feel for you. I feel sorry for you.

"Why do I feel sorry for you? Because, my friends, I know that you are throwing away the only thing that really counts!"

Jean-Marie was crying harder now. The tears poured from under his closed lids. His voice rose higher, filling the little church.

"What are you throwing away, my friends?" he cried. "As if you didn't know! You are throwing away the chance of heaven! That is what you are throwing away.

"And what is heaven, my friends? You know that too. Heaven is where one sees God face to face! Think of that, my friends. Think! Think!"

Jean-Marie's voice, still high, took on a tone of awe and wonder. "Think, my friends!" he shouted. "To see God face to face! What bliss! What overwhelming happiness!

"Yes, my friends, I know what you are asking. You are asking, 'But is it not difficult to get to heaven?' No, my friends. You can go to heaven by keeping a simple little rule. The rule is so simple that once I have told you, I know you will never forget it.

"And what is the rule? It is this: *Do only those things that are pleasing to God!*

"Think, my friends. Think! God offers you so much

and asks so little. He asks only that you live by that simple rule.

"Do only those things that are pleasing to God!"

Jean-Marie ceased speaking. He did not know why he had begun. Nor did he know why he had suddenly ceased. He knew only that the words had come to him, he had said them, and now he was through.

His eyes were still closed. He opened them slowly and in dread. He was certain that he had made a fool of himself. He was certain that he would find a mocking smile on every face before him.

But such was not the case. Instead he saw tears in the eyes of his silent congregation. Yes, tears! He could see them as plainly as a few minutes before he had felt his own coursing down his cheeks.

With a sob that was almost a whimper he bowed his head. A great and silent prayer of thanks welled along his quivering lips.

9

THE CONFESSOR

THAT SUNDAY, the Sunday on which Jean-Marie found himself speaking without difficulty from the pulpit, was a turning point in his life and in the lives of the people of Ars.

Never again did he have to memorize his sermons. He simply got up in the pulpit and spoke. He spoke easily, conversationally.

"God has created us and placed us in this world because He loves us", he said one morning. "To save our souls we must know, love, and serve God. How beautiful a life! How beautiful, how great, to know, to love, to serve God! Anything whatever that we do apart from that is a waste of time."

Thus he spoke to his people. His words and thoughts were always quite simple, but they went like arrows to the hearts of his listeners. Soon people were standing in the aisles during his Sunday Masses.

Jean-Marie was pleased, but he was not satisfied. He did not want his parishioners to be merely "Sunday Christians". He wanted them to be all-week-long Christians.

To make the church attractive to them he pushed ahead with his repairs. He was disappointed to discover that the new steeple would have to wait. The project turned out to be too costly even for wealthy Mademoiselle des Garets.

He went ahead, however, with the repairs on the lower part of the building. When those were completed he went on begging tours. He tramped the country roads for miles around. He walked to Lyon and visited wealthy people there. With the money he collected he enlarged the church, adding chapels to his favorite saints. Eventually he was able to have the wooden steeple replaced by a square tower of red brick.

By 1830, Ars had become the most completely Christian village in all France. The people no longer spent their spare hours in the cabarets; the cabarets had closed for lack of business. They no longer spent their Sundays working in the fields. They went to Mass.

On workdays too, the church was the center of their lives. When the bell sounded for evening prayer, many of the women gathered around the pulpit to make the responses to Jean-Marie. The men, coming and going from the fields during the day, slipped in to visit the Blessed Sacrament, leaving their tools at the door, their flocks waiting in the road. Stealing became almost unheard of; so did lying and gossiping.

When a whole village changes in this way, of course, other people begin to hear about it. By 1830, Jean-Marie's little church—now really a big church— had become a national shrine. From all over France pilgrims visited it, coming at the rate of between twenty and one hundred a day.

In the beginning the people came to hear Jean-Marie preach. After a while most of them came to confess to him. Yes, almost everybody wanted to confess to this simple country pastor, this awkward French peasant who had been such a slow learner that he had been forbidden to hear a single confession during the first year of his priestly life!

All kinds of people came to him: bishops and other priests, famous statesmen and hard-working farmers. They came from many miles away. They stood in line for hours, sometimes for days, waiting their turn at the confessional.

Why? Everybody asked that question, and everybody who was asked gave a different answer. Many said it was because Jean-Marie was so kind—kind, yet firm. He did not let his penitents off easily, but when he scolded them he did so with compassion, with pity. "He has suffered so much himself", one old woman said, "that he understands the sufferings of others."

One reason many gave for wishing to confess to Jean-Marie was that he could "read hearts". They pointed to many examples of this.

Entering the church at dawn one morning, Jean-Marie noticed a young woman praying at the altar rail. He had never seen her before. She was a pilgrim, newly arrived in Ars during the night.

Something about her drew his attention: her tear-stained cheeks, her troubled expression. He went to her, his hands outstretched. He lifted her to her feet and looked searchingly into her eyes.

"Yes, Mademoiselle," he said softly, "you must do what your heart tells you. You must enter a religious order."

For a time the young woman could only look at him in shocked silence. "Oh, M'sieur Curé," she whispered finally, "I have never told a living soul that I wanted to enter an order. How did you know?"

How did he know? How indeed! Jean-Marie, in fact, was as startled at what he had told the young woman as she was. He hurried away from her, mumbling to himself, "Oh, dear, oh, dear, oh, dear! How is it that sometimes I know what is going on in the heart of another person?"

That very day an old merchant from Lyon entered the confessional. The old merchant was a freethinker. He did not believe what the Church said about right and wrong; he preferred to make up his own rules about such things. He had come to Ars out of curiosity. Seeing that everyone else was going to confession, he decided to do so, too.

"And how long is it since you made your last confession?" Jean-Marie asked him.

"Thirty years", the old man replied cheerfully.

"No, my friend. It is thirty-three. Exactly thirty-three years ago this very day you made your last confession at the Notre Dame church in Lyon."

"But, M'sieur Curé, I have never seen you. You have never set eyes on me. How can you know such things about a perfect stranger?"

Jean-Marie could only sigh. All he could say was that sometimes, thanks to the grace of God, he did know such things even about strangers.

"And now", he said, "we shall go on with your confession, eh?"

The old man remained in the confessional for twenty minutes. When he left he was no longer a freethinker.

A few days later a bandit came to confession. He had not been to the sacraments for years. He was sick now. He did not have long to live. He was afraid of dying; that was what had brought him to confession. But in his heart he did not really repent his crimes.

Strangely enough, Jean-Marie knew this. He sensed that the bandit was not truly repentant the minute he began making his confession.

When the bandit had finished, Jean-Marie was silent for a while. Then, "I'm sorry for you, my friend," he said, "but since you are not really repentant, you are only wasting your time here." And he sent the man away without giving him absolution.

The bandit returned the next day. He was repentant now, but some of his crimes had been so ugly that he did not have the courage to reveal them. When he stopped speaking, Jean-Marie quietly listed for him the sins he had failed to mention. Then he gave him absolution. As for the bandit, he did not say another word. He was speechless with surprise.

With so many people crowding into the church, Jean-Marie's days were full. He went to bed at nine in the evening, sometimes later. At midnight he was up again and on his way to the church, carrying a lighted lantern.

There were always people around, even at this dark hour. They milled about in the cemetery or stood waiting on the porch Jean-Marie had had built underneath the new belltower. Making his way into the church, Jean-Marie lit a couple of tapers, said his prayers, and rang the church bells.

Then he went into the confessional. He remained

there until it was time for Mass. After Mass he ate his skimpy breakfast and returned to the confessional. Almost every day he was in it at least twelve hours, often for as long as eighteen.

He did not mind the crowds or the hard work. He did mind the people who sometimes pushed up to him to tell him to his face that he was a saint. He was still frightened of praise, of having his head turned.

He fled such people. He was happier among the defiant sinners, happiest of all in the presence of people who were just quietly doing their best to be good.

There was an old man, a citizen of Ars, who came to the church practically every day. He always behaved in the same manner. He said the Our Father and the Hail Mary on his knees, after which he simply sat in one of the pews, gazing at the figure of Christ Crucified above the altar.

The day came when Jean-Marie could no longer hold back his curiosity. "M'sieur," he said to the old man, "I see you sitting here so often, just looking at the crucifix. I can't help but wonder what is going on in your mind."

"Going on in my mind, M'sieur Curé?" The old man smiled. "Nothing. I am not much good at thinking, nor do I know many prayers. So I just sit here, as you see, looking at God. I look at Him, and He looks at me. That is all."

Jean-Marie moved away, shaking his head. He had

heard many lectures at the seminary, long and learned lectures describing how a human being might get closer to God. Never, it seemed to him, had he heard anyone explain it as well as this old man with his quiet, "I look at Him, and He looks at me."

10

SAINT PHILOMENA

IN 1819, Jean-Marie's second year at Ars, his father died at the old farmhouse in Dardilly. He left his priest-son a small inheritance. Jean-Marie put it aside. Someday, he told himself, he would use this money to do something special for the church.

Five years later, returning from a visit to a sick parishioner, he sighted three small girls walking along the country road. He had never seen the girls before.

Their appearance startled and saddened him. Their dresses were in rags. Their faces were hollow and dirty. Their eyes had the dry look that comes when one has cried to the point where there are no more tears left to shed.

Jean-Marie took the little girls home to the presbytery and questioned them closely. They were sisters, he discovered, and orphans. For months they had been wandering around the countryside, going from farm to farm, begging for food. France, they told Jean-Marie, was full of children like themselves—children left homeless as a result of the Napoleonic wars.

Now Jean-Marie knew what to do with the money his father had left him. He had a house built near the church, an orphanage and school. He called the house *La Providence* and placed in charge of it a pious young woman named Catherine Lassagne. In the beginning, Catherine had fifteen small charges. In time *La Providence* became the home of sixty orphaned girls.

For years, all went well at *La Providence*. Then came the summer of 1829. It was a bad summer for the peasants. There were fierce storms during the harvest season. As winter came on, the farmers in the Ars area had scarcely enough grain to feed their stock.

One midwinter morning, as Jean-Marie was removing his vestments after Mass, Catherine Lassagne hurried into the sacristy with a troubled face.

"M'sieur Curé!" Her voice quivered with distress. "Is it true that no grain can be purchased anywhere?"

"Not in this part of the country. Perhaps in one of the city markets—in Lyon or in Villefranche."

"And how long would it take to get grain from one of those markets?"

"A month at the very least, Catherine. Why do you ask?"

"Come with me, M'sieur. I will show you why I ask."

Catherine had already opened the sacristy door. She hurried along the path and through the gate of the stone wall with which Jean-Marie had long since replaced the old hawthorn hedge around the presbytery.

Jean-Marie followed her. In the presbytery they hurried up the stone stairs. On the second floor, Catherine flung open the door to the rear of the room, the room Jean-Marie had set aside as a granary for the orphanage.

"There!" she said, gesturing with her slender arm. "There—you see why I ask."

The room was almost empty! There was only a small pile of grain—enough, perhaps, for a dozen loaves of bread.

"*Ma Foi!*" Jean-Marie muttered. He glanced sharply at Catherine. "And there is no bread at the orphanage?"

"A few loaves, M'sieur. Enough for today, perhaps tomorrow."

"And how long have you known that we were getting low? Why was I not notified?"

"You have so much on your mind, M'sieur. Besides, the other women at the orphanage and I—we kept hoping, we prayed, we thought perhaps—perhaps a miracle . . . !"

Jean-Marie frowned. "A miracle, eh? Ah, Catherine, who are we to ask for a miracle? Still, . . ." He favored Catherine with his shy smile. "Still, it could happen. Catherine, have you ever heard of Saint François Regis?"

"But of course, M'sieur Curé. His tomb is in the mountain village of Louvesc. Do you think Saint François Regis might help us?"

"He helped me once. It was while I was studying under M'sieur Balley. I could not learn Latin, so I made a pilgrimage to Saint François Regis' tomb. I have no brains, you know. There was not much for Saint François Regis to work with. But he did his best; he helped me.

Jean-Marie paused and smiled again. "I'm not sure he will listen to me, Catherine. But the girls, the little girls, perhaps he will listen to them. Hurry to the orphanage, Catherine. Tell the children there will be no classes this morning, no catechism. Every child is to spend the morning praying to Saint François Regis. You understand me, Catherine?"

"Yes, M'sieur Curé."

"Good. Come back here at noon. And then—well, then we shall see. Be off with you now."

Catherine did as she was told. Jean-Marie went at

once to his bedroom. Among his few possessions was a statue of Saint François Regis, a small wooden figure that the Abbé Balley had given him.

Returning to the granary, he placed the statue on the floor. He heaped around it what grain there was. Dropping to his knees, he prayed as he had never prayed before.

He did not remain long in the granary. There was a line of people, he knew, waiting for him at the church. All morning he spent in the confessional. At noon he returned to the presbytery.

Catherine Lassagne was waiting for him. She leaped from one of the kitchen chairs as he entered. She was nervous, he could see. Her eyes kept shifting in the direction of the stone stairs to the second floor.

"Well, Catherine," he said, "have you looked? Have you opened the door to the granary?"

"No, M'sieur."

"And why not? Did you not pray to the good saint?"

"Yes, M'sieur Curé."

"And the children?"

"We all prayed, M'sieur. The children, the other women at the orphanage, we all prayed."

"Well, then?"

"Oh, M'sieur, I am afraid to look."

"Catherine! You have doubts?"

"I can't help it, M'sieur. I keep thinking about what you said this morning. Who are we to ask for a miracle?"

"Who indeed! But Saint François Regis is a very great saint, Catherine, and a kind one. If he asks for a miracle, there will be one. Upstairs with you now, and no more doubts."

Catherine left him. Jean-Marie paced the floor. He crossed the kitchen several times. He was beginning to think Catherine was going to spend the whole afternoon upstairs when he heard her calling to him.

He hurried up. The young woman was tugging at the granary door. "It won't open", she called to him. "It's as though something were holding it on the other side."

Jean-Marie took hold of the knob. He pulled hard. The door flew open at once, and a cataract of golden grain poured into the hallway.

The granary was full—full to the roof!

For the next few days the citizens of Ars and the pilgrims crowding into the little town talked of nothing but the granary incident. Some people said that Jean-Marie was, in truth, a saint, that he could work miracles.

When Jean-Marie heard what people were saying, he was horrified. At Mass the following Sunday he brought up the matter. He no longer talked from the pulpit. Hard work, little food, and less sleep had taken their toll. He had been ill many times. Once the doctors had all but despaired of his life. He now gave his sermons seated in a small chair with curling iron legs.

He spoke slowly this morning and in a stern voice. "My friends," he said, "I hear people saying that I have worked a miracle. This is not so. On the morning of the event I placed a statue of Saint François Regis in the granary. I prayed to him. So did the women of the orphanage and the little girls. So you see how it was. It was not I, but Saint François Regis, who obtained the grain for us. To say otherwise is to insult a great saint. I beg of you, keep this fact in mind."

He could see by the looks on their faces that most of the people did not believe him. Oh, well, there was one consoling thought. People had short memories. In a few weeks, a few months, they would forget all about the granary incident.

Things might have worked out that way except that a few months later something else happened. It was a spring morning, sparkling bright. Jean-Marie had just left the presbytery after his breakfast. With him was a young Brother, for by now the work of the parish had become too heavy for him to handle alone.

In the open space between the presbytery and the church there was an unusually large crowd. They shouted at him as he walked along. A few held out their hands. He gave them some of the medals and relics he always carried in the pocket of his soutane.

He became aware of a stir in the crowd. A young woman carrying a baby squeezed into the open space and approached him. Her face was haggard with suffering. He looked at her with pity. Tears filled his eyes as he saw the baby in her arms. There was a large and ugly tumor over one of the child's eyes.

The woman stood before him now, blocking the way. "Oh, M'sieur Curé," she said, "look at my poor child. See how he suffers."

"I see, my good woman. And I see how you suffer for him. Be comforted. Remember how our Lord suffered for us, how He taught that each of us must bear his cross—that, in fact, one's cross is his ladder to heaven."

"But, M'sieur Curé, the little one need not suffer so. You can cure him."

"Oh, no, my friend." Jean-Marie lifted a hand to protest.

"But I know you can, M'sieur. Only touch the tumor. Only touch it and my child will be well."

What could he do? He touched the tumor, telling himself that perhaps the act itself would be of some comfort to the young mother. He moved on, walking so fast that his assistant, the young Brother, could not keep up with him.

As he reached the church steps he heard a sudden commotion behind him. A woman screamed; then everyone was yelling and shouting. He turned, wondering what could have happened.

As he did so, the crowd parted. He could see the woman—the woman with the child—coming toward him. She lifted the baby, crying and laughing at the same time. "See, M'sieur Curé!" she cried. "See what you have done!"

He saw, although he had trouble believing it.

The child was cured. There was no doubt about it. The tumor was quite gone.

Jean-Marie looked wildly around him. He realized that he might not be able to credit this miracle to Saint François Regis. He had not so much as thought of him in months. Even so, Saint François Regis might have done it. If not, then some other saint. He must pray. Perhaps God would reveal the name of the saint. He must go somewhere by himself and pray. He must get away from these shouting people.

But how? The people were all around him now, like a wall. He thought of the medals and relics in his pocket. He dug out a handful and threw them high in the air so that they flew in all directions.

As he had expected, the people scattered, everybody trying to put his hands on one of the holy items. Taking advantage of the situation, Jean-Marie ran up the stairs, leaving his assistant far behind.

The church was empty. Seeing this, he did something he had never done before. He locked the front doors. Hurrying through the building, he locked the sacristy door.

Alone now, he could pray. Perhaps he could figure this thing out. Could it have been Saint François Regis? Doubtful. As far as he knew, Saint François Regis had never cured the sick.

He rushed into one of the chapels. He had thrown himself down before he quite realized where he was. It was the chapel he had built to Saint Philomena.

Saint Philomena? Could she be the one? Several cures, he reminded himself, had been attributed to her.

At this moment his thoughts about her were confused. It took him a minute to untangle them. He had built the chapel, he remembered, because she had been one of the Abbé Balley's favorites. It was the abbé who had first told him about her.

Jean-Marie remembered the occasion. The two of them, he and Monsieur Balley, had been on their way to Lyon. As they walked along, the Abbé Balley had told him the strange story of Saint Philomena, the thirteen-year-old girl who, in the first century after our Lord's death, died as a martyr to Christ in the city of Rome. Her parents buried her in one of the catacombs, those caves where the persecuted early Christians met in secret to hear the word of God. On her tomb, traced in red lead, were the words:

"Peace be with you, Philomena."

For seventeen hundred years nothing more was heard of the little martyr. Then, in 1805, her bones were removed from the grave and placed inside the statue of a young girl holding, in one hand, an arrow and, in the other, a palm and a lily.

In those days it was the custom, at times, to put clothes on a saint's statue. The Roman lady who volunteered to do this for Saint Philomena's statue had been suffering for ten years from a seemingly incurable disease. The minute her hands touched the little figure, the disease left her. Later, the statue containing Saint Philomena's relics was responsible for more cures.

As Jean-Marie thought over the few known facts about Saint Philomena, his nervousness left him. He had often prayed to the little martyr. He promised himself that in the future he would pray to her daily, for now he was quite certain that it was she who had brought the cure to the stricken baby.

On the following Sunday, seated in his chair in the sanctuary, he told his people about her. "I am convinced", he declared, "that it was her prayers, and not mine, that caused the little one's tumor to disappear."

He fervently hoped that the people would believe him. He did not want them telling him that he was a miracle worker. He was afraid such praise would make him proud and puffed up. He admired the virtue of humility, and he knew how hard it was for a priest like himself—a priest very popular with the people—to practice it.

In the months and years to come, there were more miraculous healings in Ars. Each time, at least one person came running to him, crying, "See what you have done, M'sieur Curé!" Each time, Jean-Marie made the same reply. "It was not I who did it. It was my little friend in heaven, Saint Philomena."

Did the people believe him? Jean-Marie never knew. He knew only that he believed, and that was enough.

JEAN-MARIE'S CURATE

B<small>Y</small> 1840, Jean-Marie had become so famous that pilgrims were pouring into Ars at the rate of four hundred a day. Special trains brought them from the nearby cities of Lyon, Villefranche, and Belley. In Ars the townspeople erected several hotels to shelter the ever-increasing crowds.

Most of the priests in the surrounding parishes were pleased with this development. They urged their own parishioners to visit Ars. They praised the people of Ars for setting an example of true Christian living.

Some of the priests were not pleased. They did not like the way people praised Jean-Marie and sought him out. They were jealous of him. In a village some ten miles from Ars, a young pastor got up in his pulpit one Sunday and scolded his parishioners vigorously.

"I hear", he said, "that some of you are going to Ars to make your confessions. I want you to know that I forbid this. I strictly forbid it!"

That evening the young pastor wrote a letter to Jean-Marie. The letter arrived in Ars the next day. Catherine Lassagne brought it to Jean-Marie and sat beside him, in the presbytery kitchen, while he read it.

It was an unkind letter. "My dear Monsieur Curé," it began, "I am forced to write and tell you that you disgrace your cloth. I have discovered that some of my parishioners are confessing to you instead of making their confessions to me as they should. It is shameful of you to permit this. A man who knows as little about the finer points of religion as you do ought never to enter a confessional."

Jean-Marie read the letter several times. Then he gave it to Catherine Lassagne to read. Then he sighed.

"Fetch pen and ink, Catherine", he said. "I want to dictate a reply to this letter."

"A reply, M'sieur Curé? But how can you reply? Whoever wrote this cruel letter did not have the courage to sign it!"

Jean-Marie smiled. "I know all the priests in this area, Catherine", he said. "I know their handwriting. Fetch pen and ink, please. I want to thank this young pastor for reminding me of what an unworthy man I am."

"Thank him!" Catherine Lassagne's dark face, usually so gentle, twisted with anger. "How can you thank him for writing you a mean and nasty letter full of lies?"

"There are no lies in this letter, Catherine. Every word of it is true. Fetch the pen and ink."

Shaking her head, Catherine got the pen and ink, and Jean-Marie dictated his reply. A few days later the young priest who had written the unkind letter appeared in Ars. Finding Jean-Marie in the church, he flung himself weeping at the Curé's feet.

"Oh, my good Curé," he said to Jean-Marie, "when I received your reply to my letter, I realized all at once what a great sin I had committed. I implore you to forgive me."

Jean-Marie raised the trembling man to his feet. "Please," he said, "do not ask my forgiveness. Your letter did me a great favor. You see how it is with me here. The people run after me. I felt your letter came as a penance, and no one is in greater need of penance than myself."

There were more letters, cruel, insulting—and unsigned. One spring another young pastor, in charge of one of the parishes near Ars, wrote and circulated a petition to the bishop. In his petition the young pastor described Jean-Marie as an "ignorant fool who could not even pass his final examination at the seminary". He asked the bishop to remove Jean-Marie from his pastorate.

Several priests in the area signed the petition. One of them sent it to Jean-Marie. He explained his reasons for doing so in an attached note. He felt it was only fair for Jean-Marie to know why some of his fellow priests thought he should be dismissed.

Jean-Marie read the petition carefully. Then, at the bottom of this paper which labeled him an "ignorant fool" and asked for his dismissal, he signed his own name! Then he sent the petition on to the bishop.

Ars was no longer a part of the diocese of Lyon. It was now in the diocese of Belley, another of the nearby cities. The Bishop of Belley was an old man, wise and kindly. After reading the petition, he sent two of his assistants to Ars to look into matters there. The two assistants returned shortly.

"The Curé of Ars, my lord," one of them said, "is nothing less than a saint."

The Bishop of Belley nodded. He had thought as much. In due time he got together some of the priests who had signed the petition against Jean-Marie.

"My sons," he told them, "it is wise at times for us who are priests to remind ourselves that we are still human beings. Even our hearts are sometimes tainted by the terrible sin of envy. As for the Curé of Ars, I ask you one question: Do you really think you are furthering the work of God when you send him anonymous letters and circulate petitions against him?"

The old bishop fell silent for a moment. Then, smiling sadly, he proceeded. "Would it not be better", he asked the priests, "for you to imitate what you call the 'foolish ways' of the Curé of Ars? My assistants tell me that he is a saint. I myself believe this to be the case."

After that, Jean-Marie received no more cruel letters. No more petitions were circulated against him. But his troubles were not over.

By 1845, his work had become so heavy that the Bishop of Belley sent him a curate. The curate, Monsieur Raymond, was a vigorous man in the prime of life. He was tall, broad-shouldered, and handsome. He spoke Latin beautifully and had been a first-class student at the seminary. In short, Monsieur Raymond was everything that Jean-Marie was not.

At the altar Jean-Marie wore only the finest of vestments. But his personal clothes were rags and tatters. Year in and year out he wore the same worn soutane, the sash of which had long since disappeared. He wore the same battered three-cornered hat, or, rather, he carried it under his arm, for he rarely appeared with a hat on.

Monsieur Raymond, on the other hand, wore only the most elegant of clerical garments.

Then too, Jean-Marie had no system about anything. He simply got up in the middle of the night and went about his pastoral duties, whatever they were. He heard confessions, he said Mass, he visited the sick, he went on begging tours. Occasionally he conducted a mission in some neighboring parish. He was always busy, but he never did things in any particular order.

Monsieur Raymond, on the other hand, was the soul of order. Shortly after his arrival in Ars, he had ropes set up in front of the church. He saw to it that persons going to confession entered the church according to a certain system, the men at one time of the day, the women at another.

He was forever issuing bulletins and lists of rules. Nor did he sign these announcements "Monsieur Raymond, Curate", as he should have. He signed them "Monsieur Raymond, Pastor".

Catherine Lassagne spoke to Jean-Marie about this. "M'sieur Curé," she said angrily, "you must stop Monsieur Raymond from signing himself 'pastor'. He is only the assistant here. You are the pastor."

"Oh, what does it matter?" was Jean-Marie's reply.

Catherine Lassagne knew better than to press the matter further. She knew that it really made no difference to Jean-Marie how Monsieur Raymond signed his bulletins and lists of rules.

Hardly a day went by that Monsieur Raymond did not come to Jean-Marie with some complaint or criticism.

"My dear Curé," he said one morning, "you really should get yourself some new clothes. A man in your position should not go around in such rags."

"Truly, I do look awful", Jean-Marie agreed; but, of course, he did nothing whatsoever about it.

Another morning it was finances. "Monsieur Curé," Monsieur Raymond said to Jean-Marie, "thousands of pilgrims come here every month, but many of them leave almost nothing in the collection boxes."

"Perhaps they are poor", Jean-Marie suggested in a mild voice.

"And perhaps", his young curate said, "it is because you do not give any real money sermons. You are forever scolding them about their sins. Why not scold them some Sunday morning for failure to put money in the collection boxes? Such a sermon would wake them up."

"Indeed it would", Jean-Marie agreed. "I will give such a sermon serious thought." He did give it thought; but he never gave the sermon.

Toward the end of his first year at Ars, Monsieur Raymond persuaded Jean-Marie to give up his big bedroom on the second floor of the presbytery.

"After all," he told Jean-Marie, "why should an old man like you have to go up and down those hard stone stairs? You will be just as comfortable in the little bedroom on the first floor. Am I not right?"

"Whatever you say, Monsieur Raymond", said Jean-Marie.

"Good!" Monsieur Raymond nodded brightly, his dark curls dancing. "I will have your bed moved downstairs at once."

"Oh, don't trouble", said Jean-Marie. "I can sleep on the floor."

For many months he did just that. He threw a blanket on the stones of the first-floor bedroom, and that was his bed. It was a dark, damp room, scarcely larger than a closet. Upstairs Monsieur Raymond piled Jean-Marie's old bed high with blankets and made himself cozy.

The townspeople heard about this, of course. At first they merely muttered among themselves. Then one day, Monsieur Mandy, the mayor, got together a committee of townspeople and called on Monsieur Raymond.

Monsieur Mandy did the talking for his committee. "My good curate," he said to young Raymond, "we have come to say two things to you. First of all, we want you to put M'sieur Curé back in his own bedroom."

Monsieur Raymond started to speak, but the mayor did not let him. He went right on. "Secondly," he said, "we want you to stop pretending to be the pastor."

"But, sir," Monsieur Raymond put in, "you know that Jean-Marie is not capable of running a parish. He has no brains."

The mayor silenced Monsieur Raymond with a lifted hand. "We are not fools, M'sieur", he said. "We are aware that the Curé is a simple man. We know, too, that God gave you good brains and intended you to use them. Very well! A really intelligent man knows that in God's eyes the Curé's saintliness is far more important than your intelligence."

With this the mayor and his committee departed. They had got what they had come for, however. That night Jean-Marie was back in his own bedroom. As for Monsieur Raymond, he could not bear the thought of sleeping in the dark first-floor room; he found himself a pleasant room in a private home in the village.

All of these matters were known to the Bishop of Belley. Finally, after Monsieur Raymond had been at Ars for eight years, the bishop sent him to another parish. He replaced him with a young priest who loved Jean-Marie, who never criticized him, and who did everything in his power to make him comfortable.

At first Jean-Marie was relieved. After a time, however, he found himself missing Monsieur Raymond. He said as much one afternoon to Catherine Lassagne.

Catherine looked at him with amazement in her dark eyes. "You miss Monsieur Raymond!" she exclaimed. "I don't see how you could. Personally, I was overjoyed to see him go."

Jean-Marie shook his head. "Oh, no, Catherine", he said. "M'sieur Raymond was good for me."

"'Good' for you! What did he ever do but criticize you and make your life miserable?"

"Exactly. God sent me Monsieur Raymond as a penance. You know the ancient truth, Catherine. Sometimes God tests those He loves with many trials. As long as M'sieur Raymond was here, I knew that God loved me. Now I am not so sure."

Catherine Lassagne heaved an enormous sigh and shook her head. In her mind there were no doubts about God's attitude toward Jean-Marie. God greatly loved the simple, shabby, humble Curé of Ars.

12

TEMPTATIONS

ONE NIGHT during Jean-Marie's sixth year in Ars a strange thing happened in his low-ceilinged bedroom on the second floor of the presbytery. He had been asleep only a few minutes when he was awakened by a series of low patters. The patter-patter sound grew nearer, becoming louder.

Rats! Jean-Marie thought, sitting bolt upright.

His bed was a four-poster, curtained all around.

Even as the thought of rats came to him, he saw that the curtains were quivering. He heard a loud gnawing sound as if one of the beasts had climbed the curtain and was eating away a big hole.

Pushing the curtains apart, Jean-Marie leaped from the bed. He lighted his lantern and looked around. The sound continued, the light patters and the loud gnawing, but he could see nothing. He examined every inch of the curtains. He could not find so much as a single tear.

Hurrying downstairs, he got a pitchfork. Returning, he scraped at the stone floor and the wooden walls. Nothing; he could see no signs of anything. Exhausted, he returned to his bed. But he was not to sleep that night, for the sounds continued.

Off and on, for the next thirty-five years, Jean-Marie was to endure many such terrifying nights. The rat sounds never returned, but other and more unearthly sounds invaded his room and disturbed his rest.

One night he was awakened by a dreadful din that seemed to come from the yard outside the window. It was as if a pack of howling wolves had gathered there. He hurried over, but the light of his lantern, held out the window, revealed only an empty yard. Once, his bed was moved across the room. Once, the curtains were torn from their posts. One night he awakened to find them burned to ashes.

The Viscount of Ars, the brother of Mademoiselle des Garets, presented the church with a collection of valuable jewels. Until a place could be built for them in the church, Jean-Marie stored them in a cupboard at the presbytery.

That very night he was awakened by a loud and hollow pounding on the front door downstairs. His first thought, of course, was of burglars. Quite likely some burglar had heard that the jewels were in the presbytery.

Grabbing his lantern, he flew downstairs. He opened the front door. There was no one there. A heavy snow had fallen during the earlier part of the night. He held his lantern high, expecting to see footprints. There were none!

The next night he hired two men to stay in the presbytery and guard the jewels. Again he was awakened by a loud and hollow pounding on the front door. By the time he reached the lower floor, the two men had the front door open. They were examining the snow with their lanterns. As on the night before, there was no sign that anyone had been there!

The larger of the two men spoke first. "M'sieur Curé," he said, blessing himself rapidly, "we all know about those strange events here. We have often heard the sounds ourselves. I do not like to say this, M'sieur Curé, but we do not believe it is a burglar who visits you at night. We believe it is the Devil himself!"

Jean-Marie could only nod. He himself had long since decided that the weird happenings in his room were the work of the fallen angel.

"But why?" he asked Catherine Lassagne the next day. "Why does the *grappin* bother me in this way?" (*Grappin* was his nickname for the Devil.)

"Everyone knows the answer to that", Catherine replied. "The Devil knows that you have snatched countless souls from his hands. You have brought many people back to God. Naturally the Devil hates you more than he does most of us. He is trying to rob you of the little sleep you allow yourself. He hopes to wear you down."

Again Jean-Marie could only nod. He had suspected this was the case.

A few nights later he was certain. This time he was awakened by a voice, a voice that came at him between roars of cackling laughter.

"Vianney! Vianney!" the voice shrieked, addressing Jean-Marie by his last name. "Potato eater! Potato eater!" the voice went on, referring to the fact that Jean-Marie lived, for the most part, on nothing but milk and boiled potatoes.

Jean-Marie was not the least bit frightened. He had become used to the Devil. "You know," he said to Catherine Lassagne one day, "if the *grappin* stopped visiting me, I believe I would miss him. Over the years he and I have become quite good comrades."

A few nights later the cackling voice came again. It assailed Jean-Marie's ears with the same words, "Vianney! Vianney! Potato eater! Potato eater!"

This time Jean-Marie decided to answer back. "Oh,

go away, *Grappin*", he shouted. "I always thought you were clever, but these silly noises of yours are not clever at all. They are really very childish!"

Jean-Marie's shout brought an unexpected response. There were no more words. All he heard was a low, grinding sound like the gnashing of teeth.

"Ah," he told himself, "the Devil is conceited. He does not like my calling him childish. I have hurt his pride. Perhaps now he will leave me alone!"

But the Devil had no intention of leaving Jean-Marie alone. Having failed to wear him down with noises in the night, he tackled him another way.

Like many good men, Jean-Marie thought of himself as a terrible sinner. Often a frightful thought seized him, the thought that when he died God would not consider him worthy of heaven.

It was his secret fear, but the Devil knew all about it. The Devil knew, and one day he took advantage of it. As Jean-Marie sat in his confessional, the Devil saw to it that a disturbing thought entered his mind.

Jean-Marie thought about the long hours he spent hearing confessions. He thought about the crowds of people that were always around him. He knew that he was helping God to save many souls. But what about his own soul? It had been months—years, in fact—since he had had time even to think about it.

Then and there Jean-Marie decided to flee Ars and its crowds, to go away to some quiet place where he could devote his time to saving his own soul.

He said nothing about his plans. He knew that if the people of Ars learned that he wanted to leave, they would find some way to prevent him. He simply slipped away one dark night. He tramped across the bridge and along the road leading out of Ars.

He had no destination in mind. His plan was to keep walking until he found a quiet place—some monastery, perhaps—where he could live the rest of his life in silence and in prayer.

He walked on and on. The false dawn came and, suddenly, in its wavering light, Jean-Marie saw a tall cross standing in the middle of the road before him. He stopped dead still. He stood thus for some time; then he turned around and returned to Ars.

"I cannot really say what came over me", he told Catherine Lassagne later. "It was as if our Lord were standing there, blocking my way. I got the feeling that He wanted me to return here and go on with my work."

The Devil had lost a second time; but the Devil does not give up easily. Three more times Jean-Marie fled Ars. Once he got as far as his old home in Dardilly.

There he made a discovery. He could not flee crowds. When the people learned where he was, they came to Dardilly. He awakened one morning to find the farmyard filled with shouting people, demanding that he hear their confessions. That afternoon he returned to Ars by coach.

He never attempted to flee again. "What a fool I've been", he confided to Catherine. "How silly of me not to understand that it was the Devil who wanted me to flee Ars. After all, I am a priest. I cannot go where I please, when I please. A priest cannot hope to save his soul by breaking his vows of obedience to Mother Church."

Jean-Marie was very old now. His long, curling hair was snow-white. Years of hard work, many illnesses, the sacrifices he had undergone—these things had reduced him to mere skin and bones. He had made his last journey on this earth, but his final journey—his journey to God—was not far distant.

AFTERWORD

On the morning of August 3, 1859—a frightfully hot day—Jean-Marie Baptiste Vianney died in the old stone presbytery at Ars. Thousands of people attended his funeral Mass. They wept and whispered among themselves. "He was a saint", they said.

In 1872, the Church of God gave Jean-Marie the title of Venerable. Years later, in 1905, he was given the title of Blessed and made "patron of all priests having charge of souls in France." Finally, on November 1, 1924, Pope Pius XI, speaking in the presence of two hundred bishops and thirty-five cardinals, declared him to be what many who had known him in life had always said he was, a saint!

Among the many biographies of Saint Jean-Marie is one by the French dramatist Henri Ghéon. Ghéon calls his biography *The Secret of the Curé of Ars.*

What was the secret? How was it that this simple French farmer, who could not even pass his seminary examinations, could become so fine a priest and so great a saint?

An old story about the thirteenth-century Christian philosopher Saint Thomas Aquinas may explain it in part.

Near the University of Paris, where Saint Thomas Aquinas worked as a professor, was a small community of nuns. One day the Mother Superior gathered her nuns together and put them to work making a book.

For the pages of the book the finest of vellum was purchased. The pages were stitched together and placed between a leather binding on which the nuns had tooled a beautiful design. Then the Mother Superior carried the book to Saint Thomas Aquinas.

"When you open this book," she told him, "you will see that the pages are blank. On these pages I want you to write the great secret—the rules by which my nuns can get to heaven."

"Reverend Mother," Saint Thomas Aquinas replied, "I shall be glad to do this for you."

Mother Superior returned to her community. There she and her nuns resigned themselves to a long wait. They assumed that it would take Saint Thomas Aquinas many months, perhaps years, to write such an important book.

But in this they were mistaken. The very next day Saint Thomas Aquinas appeared, bringing the book.

"What!" Mother Superior said to him. "You have already written it?"

"Yes, Mother Superior," Saint Thomas Aquinas said, "I have finished it." And he went away.

Now Mother Superior and her nuns would know

the great secret, the rules for getting to heaven. With trembling hands they opened the book—and gasped! Saint Thomas Aquinas had written only two words.

"Will it!" he had written.

Yes, that seems to have been the secret of the simple Curé of Ars. He willed to go to heaven, and, in the words of the First Grand Vicar of Lyon, the grace of God did the rest!

AUTHOR'S NOTE

Most of the biographies on which this story is based were written by men who knew the Curé of Ars in his lifetime or who obtained their information by interviewing people who did. Chief among those consulted were *Life of the Curé of Ars* by Abbé Alfred Monnin (Baltimore: Kelly and Piet, 1865), *A Saint in the Making* by John A. Oxenham (Longmans, 1931), and *The Secret of the Curé of Ars* by Henri Ghéon (Longmans, 1929).

Other sources, consulted for background purposes, were chapters dealing with Ars in the book *Miracles* by Jean Helle (David McKay, 1952), *France of the French* by Edward Harrison Barker (Scribner's, 1909), the sections devoted to France in *Shepherds of Britain* by Adelaide L. J. Gosset (London: Constable, 1911), miscellaneous guide-books on France written during the Curé's lifetime, miscellaneous publications in the Map Room of the New York Public Library, and the *Catholic Encyclopedia* and *Encyclopædia Britannica* accounts of the French Revolution and the Napoleonic era.

The little French village of Ars, where the Curé

had his church, is still a world-famous shrine, visited by thousands of pilgrims every year. The Mathias Loras who figures in the book as a classmate of the Curé emigrated to the United States in 1829 and on December 10, 1837, was consecrated first Bishop of Dubuque, Iowa.

In the Catholic churches of France, especially in the rural areas, statues of the Curé of Ars are commonplace. Such is not the case in the United States. There is a statue of the Curé at St. Agnes' on East Forty-third Street, New York City, but apparently few others. The wonder is that there are not more, for in the long and brilliant history of the saints there are few figures more lovable or more appealing than Saint Jean-Marie Baptiste Vianney, the humble country priest who had great difficulty learning his Latin but who readily out-talked the Devil.